elia's first urge was to make run for it...

...through the restaurant and out the door before Nick Avery arrived. There were lots of exits from Rockefeller Plaza—whoever was following her couldn't be at all of them, unless he wasn't alone. Still, she'd be playing Russian roulette with escape routes.

She tried to think what would be the best, the safest alternative, but her mind refused to cooperate. All she could think about was how Nick's voice on the phone had thrilled through her like a sudden shattering of glass.

She reminded herself that she was in trouble...she needed help...she needed protection....

But did she need Nick Avery?

Dear Reader,

Sometime, somewhere, any woman might need protection. And who could be more sexy—or dangerous—than her bodyguard? You're about to meet another bodyguard employed by the fictional agency Protection Enterprises Incorporated.

This month Alice Orr brings you *Protect Me, Love,* the third and final book in the MY BODYGUARD subseries. This is Alice's seventh Intrigue novel. It is set in New York City where Alice lives and toward which she feels both affection and trepidation. Both are apparent in this story of passion and danger in the extreme.

In addition to her writing life, Alice is a literary agent, wife and mother. She also lectures nationally on writing and publishing. You can write her at Alice Orr Agency, Inc., 305 Madison Avenue, Suite 1166, New York, NY 10165. You may also E-mail Alice at <orragency@aol.com>.

At Harlequin Intrigue, we know you'll enjoy *Protect Me, Love,* and hope you'll read the past titles in the MY BODYGUARD subseries: #391 *Guarded Moments* by Cassie Miles and #394 *Shadow Lover* by Carly Bishop. Don't miss the MY BODYGUARD series!

Sincerely,

Debra Matteucci
Senior Editor and Editorial Coordinator
Harlequin Books
300 East 42nd Street
New York, New York 10017

Protect Me, Love
Alice Orr

Harlequin Books

TORONTO • NEW YORK • LONDON
AMSTERDAM • PARIS • SYDNEY • HAMBURG
STOCKHOLM • ATHENS • TOKYO • MILAN
MADRID • WARSAW • BUDAPEST • AUCKLAND

To my husband, Jonathan, always my romantic hero.
To Ed Vesneske, my beloved son.
To my precious confidant, Kathleen Zea, also my dear
daughter.
To my editor, Julianne Moore, a true jewel.
To my agent, Rob Cohen,
a savvy voice in a wacky world.

ISBN 0-373-22398-6

PROTECT ME, LOVE

Copyright © 1996 by Alice Orr

Printed in U.S.A.

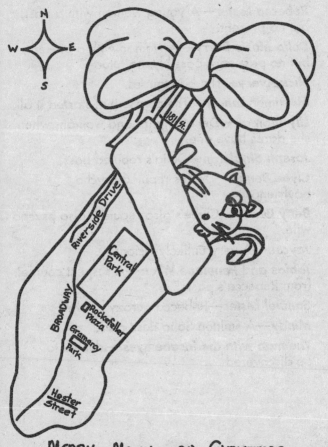

MERRY MANHATTAN CHRISTMAS—

—Alice

CAST OF CHARACTERS

Rebecca Lester—A young woman with a past, but no present.

Delia Marie Barry—A woman with a present, but no past and, possibly, no future.

Nick Avery—The bodyguard.

Mortimer Lancer—The corpse that started it all.

Lily Tubman—Delia's right-hand woman, when she dares have one.

Joseph Singleton—Delia's reputed boss.

Clyde Benno—Delia's reputed psycho boyfriend.

Betty Benno—Clyde's also reputed, also psycho wife.

Jaycee—A very unlikely visionary.

Tobias and Penelope Wren—A suspect couple from Rebecca's past.

Samuel Lester—Rebecca's crazy brother.

Mindy—A smitten Soho desk clerk.

The man with the insane eyes—Identity to be discovered.

Prologue

Becky Lester of Denver, Colorado, woke up with Nick Avery on her mind. For the first time in four years, she felt almost completely happy. Because of that, she didn't let herself return to consciousness right off. She kept the feeling of Nick in her heart, as if she were still dreaming of him, the way he'd looked that day in the study of the main house of the Lester estate. She'd seen him many times before, of course, when he'd first started working as a bodyguard for her father. She simply hadn't noticed Nick as a man—as a highly desirable man—until that particular moment, maybe because she needed to notice him, because now she needed a fantasy.

She'd been rushing past the study, late as usual to some hot evening that wouldn't turn out to be so hot after all. Nick was talking to Mortimer Lancer, the Lester family lawyer and chief trustee of the estate. Becky had passed the open doorway before she registered what she'd seen. She backtracked then, and Nick must have heard her because he turned around. That was the moment the dream of him began. He was built exactly the way she liked a man to be—tall and rangy with long-muscled thighs, tight in the hips, wide and

hard at the shoulders. He also obviously didn't mind
letting that show. Otherwise, he wouldn't have had on
close-fitting jeans and a blue chambray shirt that
stretched taut across his ample chest. And that was only
his body. His face was just right for fantasy, too—dark
brows over eyes arrogant enough to be a challenge; a
mouth that all but said out loud, "I want to kiss you
right this minute," and thick, somewhat overlong, dark
hair that was meant to be tousled on a woman's pillow.

Becky took all of this in, that particular day, along
with the way her knees were threatening to forget their
function of holding her upright. In response she locked
those knees tight. She did her best most of the time to
make people think she was all fluff between the ears,
but she drew the line at actually feeling that way herself. Yet, at that moment, she'd have sworn she had
cotton candy for brains. All of a sudden, Nick Avery
had made her feel like that, and she wasn't sure whether
this was good or bad.

Meanwhile, he'd been giving her the once-over, too.
She was decked out in one of her deliberately bimboid
outfits—too tight, too short and too black for a sensible woman to wear. He slid his gaze over her. She all but
shivered, and not because she had too few clothes on in
the still chilly Colorado springtime. Of course, he
probably thought she was on the skinny side. Most men
told her so, but she couldn't help that. It had been well
over three years since she was able to get a full meal
down and keep it there. She hoped Nick might think she
was pretty anyway. Or, maybe it was enough for her to
look at how gorgeous he was and daydream about it,
obsess over it, hang on to it.

Over the several weeks since, she'd played that fantasy out like a Colorado River fishing line. It gave her

something to think about besides the way, three-plus years ago, her beloved father had died, her stepmother along with him. There was nobody left now, except maybe Morty Lancer, the housekeeper Penelope Wren and her caretaker husband Tobias, to care whether Becky had a dream in her head or not. She had a brother, Samuel, but he was tucked away in a mental institution. She wasn't allowed to see him much because of how upset he got when she was around, and she could barely remember the time before he was put away. He resented her so intensely that she couldn't include him in the very short list of people who gave a damn about her anyway. The last time she saw him, he'd scowled like he wanted to kill her, then chucked a vase at her head. Luckily, he'd missed, but she hadn't missed the hatred in his eyes. She'd decided right then that she didn't have a brother, not really, and she wrote him out of any corner he might have claimed in her heart.

All of which made Becky feel even more alone and ripe for an imaginary infatuation with the heartthrob bodyguard. She'd flirted with Nick in the weeks since that day in the study, but even her most vampy smiles and teasing comments got her nowhere. He was too much of a standup guy to get involved with the boss's daughter, even when the boss wasn't around any longer. Still, just thinking about him made her stretch long and lazy like a cat as she gradually awoke to another Colorado morning. She was coming out of that stretch when her arm hit something hard beneath the sheet on the other side of the bed. For a delicious instant she wondered if her fantasy had come to life and Nick was beside her. She rolled toward that impossible dream with her lips parted to receive a kiss as her eyes drifted open.

What Becky saw froze her to stone. She sat up fast, too shocked to scream. A man's arm protruded from under the sheet and dangled off the opposite side of the bed. She could tell just from looking at the angle of the arm that he was dead. She could also tell by the flabbiness of the skin that he wasn't Nick Avery. She reached over and grabbed the sheet, flipping the fabric aside to reveal what lay underneath. It was a man's body all right, and he was nude. His skin was so white it would have been pallid even while he was alive, with rolls of extra flesh under his arms and around his waist where Nick was lean and hard. This man's back was to her. Still, with the first lucid thought she was able to piece together in her paralyzed mind, she realized that she knew him.

She would have rolled him over so she could see his face, but she couldn't stand to touch what she sensed would be a cold corpse. She could get up and walk around to his side of the bed, but she was too frightened to move that far just yet. Instead, she eased herself up onto her knees, clutching her side of the sheet to her chest, suddenly modest in the presence of this poor, lifeless man. She leaned over far enough away not to touch any part of him but sufficiently close to see his face. She clamped her hand over her mouth. The sheet slipped from her body as a muffled scream made a strangled sound behind her fingers. As she'd thought, the dead man next to her was Morty Lancer. His eyes were open and staring at the opposite wall. His mouth was open, too, as if in surprise, and there was a bloody gash in his chest.

Becky doubled over with her head between her knees and gulped mouthfuls of air to fight the spasms in her stomach. Those spasms wrenched through her for a long, tortuous moment, until her stunned psyche began to comprehend the significance of Morty being dead and naked in her bed. Gradually, she straightened into a kneeling posture. Her hand moved from her mouth and drifted out in front of her as if on marionette strings. That was when her brain finally unscrambled what might have been the scariest message of all. Her hand and forearm were spotted with blood. She allowed herself the fleeting, desperate conclusion that she had touched the bloody body just now and that would explain the stains on herself, but of course that didn't make sense. She hadn't allowed herself to touch him.

Becky rolled slowly off her knees to a sitting position on the bed. She stared at her hand till her stomach started to retch again and she had to look away. That was when she saw the knife. It was lying on the pale peach rug at her side of the bed, the thick rug she liked so well on winter mornings when this huge stone house could be chilly as a tomb. The pale rug fibers bore the same stains that marked her hand and arm.

Becky leaned over to see the knife more clearly. The blade was long, and the wooden handle showed a distinct palm print in crimson. She stared at that palm print for a moment, then down at her own hand while thoughts formed themselves in her head, like titles on a movie screen. The words were stark black on a white background as her mind snapped with a jarring jolt from its shocked state into sudden alertness. She realized then, with undeniable certainty, that the print on that knife was hers.

"My God," she blurted out loud. "I killed him."

The sound of her voice lurched her to an even sharper level of alertness, and she knew at once that what she'd said wasn't true. She'd gone to sleep alone last night, and she hadn't awakened till a moment ago when her idyllic dream of infatuation ended and this horrible nightmare began. Her next thought was even clearer. If she hadn't killed Morty, then she was being set up to make it look as if she did. The pieces fell together into what might have been a paranoid conspiracy theory if she hadn't suddenly been so sure it was true.

She'd had an argument with Morty just the other day about letting her borrow on her trust fund because she'd overspent her allowance. They'd had that same argument at least a hundred times before. This time, however, they happened to be outside the pool house with several people listening in. Becky had even said Morty made her so exasperated that sometimes she wanted to kill him. That, along with the generally reckless way she lived her life these days, added up to pegging Becky as number one suspect.

She sighed what was nearly a sob and nodded her head. Somebody was setting her up, all right. She even knew what their motive would be. Her full inheritance was coming to her in a few months when she turned twenty-five. With Morty no longer around to protect her legal interests and with her out of the way in prison or on death row, a lot of people were destined to make out like bandits. Especially one person, who was crazy enough to think up a deal like this one and maybe smart enough to carry it out, too. But there was no time to think about her brother Samuel now. She had to get herself out of this mess.

Becky swung her feet over the side of the bed and stood up slowly. She was dizzy, and her legs quivered under her. She was also standing very near the knife blade. She suppressed the urge to leap away in disgust. She had to steady herself all over. If she didn't think straight now, she could spend the rest of her life, however short a duration that might be, paying for it. She had to depend on herself now, not even her fantasy Nick could help her. He was an ex-cop, after all. He'd look at this room and her and come to one conclusion, that she was guilty as sin. He'd think she'd lured Morty to her bed then murdered him. Becky was definitely on her own with no more time for daydreams.

She needed a plan, a plan for her escape. From that morning on, Rebecca Radley Lester and the life she'd known would have to be history. As she walked shakily across the carpet to her bathroom to wash the blood from her hands, Becky could already feel the emptiness of loss widening inside her—the loss of her home, her friends, her identity, and of Nick Avery, too.

Chapter One

Five years later

Delia Marie Barry enjoyed Christmas in Manhattan. Everybody was always in a hurry here, but at this time of year there was a happy, expectant quality to their haste. When she let herself be swept along by the crowd on Fifth Avenue, the lightness of her feet lifted the weight from the part of her that had been heavy-hearted for the past five years. She could almost believe she was a normal person again, with a family to buy gifts for and a full life awaiting her at home. The images that haunted her dreams were replaced for the moment by the red, green, and gold of the season. She opened up her usually carefully guarded self and let in the bright storefronts and the glitter of moving display windows populated by bustling elves and sky-treading reindeer. She let herself believe she was a child again and Santa would be coming very soon.

In Delia's five years as a New Yorker, she hadn't seen many white Christmases, though the cold was certainly sharp here in winter. This was one of those frigid days. She was glad she'd worn her long, heavy coat, the one that made her look like a version of King Wenceslas.

She held the hem closed to shield her ankles against the wind, knifing down Fifth Avenue as a reminder that December was in full tilt and Christmas only days away. Still, this wasn't the winter she'd once known, roaring off the Rocky Mountains onto the Colorado plateau, burying the world in deep white as pure as the holiday promise of a new beginning each year.

Delia ducked her head and told herself the sudden stinging in her eyes was from the wind. That was the trouble with the holidays. They made her remember, and memory was not her friend. She was an Easterner now, with her previous history submerged beneath an avalanche of necessity. She kept that mountain of subterfuge intact every day. Her safety, her very life, depended on maintaining her new persona. She even felt like she actually was that creation now, a native of this revved-up, fast paced, snapped-to-attention city she'd adopted as protective camouflage.

Even so, something of the tourist remained beneath her carefully constructed urbanite facade, along with the yearning to be as ordinary as all of these bustling people with their over-full shopping bags and long lists of places to go and things to do. It was those not quite submerged remnants of her former self that pushed Delia through the revolving door into Saks Fifth Avenue on the tide of the lunch hour rush. The first floor of Saks at holiday time was a sight to behold, with the most beautiful treasures of all civilization—silks and scents, jewels and twinkling crystal, luxuriant lotions and perfumes from Paris—in glorious array as if before a queen. Suddenly, if only for a single reckless instant, she was Becky Lester again with a bank account that could circle the globe and her own long list of people to find gifts for.

At the first jewelry counter, she pushed herself out of the streaming aisle of shoppers, drawn by the sparkle of precious gems like a chilled wanderer to fire. She'd accumulated high-ticket baubles like these herself in that other life, filled a safe full of velvet-lined trays with them. Then, they'd been a form of security, the diamond-hard proof that she had some value in the world. They'd turned out to be another kind of security, even salvation, when that world came crashing down on her one terrifying morning five years ago. She'd fled with what she could carry, a change of clothes and the contents of those velvet-lined trays dumped into a gym bag.

On that fateful morning, Delia also took with her the possibility of staying free and alive. She would be safe as long as she was careful to keep the connection severed between a headstrong, flamboyant young fugitive from a murder charge and the no-nonsense woman she'd since become. Still, there was a hint of her former self left as she bent over the jewelry case, dazzled for an instant by its sparkle. She was, of course, not recognizable as Becky. She'd been anorexic thin five years ago. She was heavier and healthier now, with flesh and curves she'd never hoped to have back then. She was also dark-haired rather than blond, with her hair grown past her shoulders instead of spiky short.

Even more drastic was the transformation in her style and bearing. She'd been prone to zingy little outfits in those days, lots of midriff showing in summer and tight leather in winter. By contrast, Delia Marie Barry had a closetful of tailored suits, all chic and flattering but definitely strictly business. Even the way she carried herself had undergone a drastic change. Self-possessed and purposeful, that's what her city sidewalk stride said about her today. She hadn't darted restlessly from one place to the next since the day circumstance set her on a path so crammed with things to watch out for and take care of that there was hardly a second left for restlessness. The only place she let the more zany side of herself loose these days was in her mind, and maybe once in a while at the Hester Street Settlement House where she volunteered as often as possible.

She allowed herself only one slim connection with her past. It was there on her right hand now, pressed against the glass of the Saks Fifth Avenue display case. She'd taken off her gloves and stuffed them into her coat pocket as she passed through the revolving door. On the smallest finger of that hand she wore the tiny ring given to her by her mother just before she died. Delia was fourteen then, ten years away from calling herself by that name. She'd never worn the ring for fear of losing it. She'd tucked it into the bottom of the first of those velvet trays that would one day fill a wall safe nearly to the top. She'd kept it hidden, hers alone to look at and cherish. The narrow golden band of interwoven aspen leaves was the only piece of jewelry she didn't sell five years ago. She'd slipped it on her finger instead, the one memento she allowed herself to keep herself tethered, however tenuously, to some history of herself. Otherwise she feared she might break loose from earth entirely and be set adrift in a universe where nobody, not even herself, could ever know who she really was. That tiny anchor sparkled now, in the discreetly modulated light of Christmas at Saks, for everyone to see.

DELIA TURNED out to be a natural for the bodyguard business. She'd spent the last years of her Denver life shadowed constantly. She was a wealthy young heiress then, a prime target for kidnappers and con artists.

She'd also been so rebellious that she wouldn't allow herself to be accompanied directly. The men assigned to her protection had to follow her around. In that period, from the deaths of her father and stepmother in a fiery helicopter crash in the Rockies to the morning of her escape from an inevitable homicide charge, she'd learned every possible way to evade her bodyguard. She'd also learned a lot about the protection business just by watching them watching her.

Delia knew the world of the wealthy and powerful from the inside out, how they live, how they think, what they require. Five years ago, when she'd needed a business to go into, personal security was tailor-made for her. She'd sold her jewelry for enough to get started, and keep going until Protective Enterprises Incorporated became profitable, with something left over to invest. The trick was to accomplish all of that while maintaining the low profile necessary to avoid detection by whoever might still be after her—the police, the Lester family, the person or persons who'd set her up for a very long fall in the first place. Her cover had to be deep and flawless.

Delia Marie Barry—office manager, assignment coordinator, functionary extraordinaire—was the answer. As far as anybody knew, Delia ran the company for a fictitious gentleman named Joseph Singleton. Meanwhile, PEI's Total Confidentiality System gave her an excuse for being secretive. Nobody other than Delia and the bodyguard himself knew what services an individual customer had contracted for or why. Thus, Delia kept one hand from knowing what the other was doing while her cover story remained comfortably intact. Her obsession with secrecy turned out to be very good for business, as well. The wealthy and powerful live in fear of robbers, kidnappers, extortionists, and swindlers, of enemies in general, and visibility makes them targets. PEI offered the closest thing to anonymity they could find. In less than three years, PEI was far enough into the black to afford the fancy Rockefeller Center address, which attracted steady customers.

Delia strolled the block from Saks to 30 Rockefeller Center, almost secure in the belief that the Total Confidentiality System protected both her clients and herself. Almost secure, but not quite.

Chapter Two

Delia thought of herself as having a three hundred sixty degree awareness. She'd trained herself to be especially vigilant on foot, so much so that she sometimes missed out on what she might be looking *at* because of what she had to be intent upon looking *for*. Some might have said she could relax now. Five years had passed without incident. She'd even weathered that touchy situation last fall when one of Morty Lancer's twin daughters came to PEI to have her sister guarded for a while. Delia'd given an Academy Award performance, and no one ever made the connection between her and Morty. Still, she tried to be on her toes every minute whether she liked living that way or not. The truth was, sometimes she got so sick of her life she wanted to scream. She didn't do that, of course. Screaming attracted too much attention, and the best security device was to keep yourself from being noticed. So she did her screaming on the inside.

The worst part was not being able to get close to anybody because that would require too much trust on her part. Trust had been her watchword for so long she sometimes wondered if she'd be able to trust anybody now at all. All of which made for a lonely life she might not have been able to stand if it weren't for her work. She filled her life with her business. She kept herself at it long and hard. She'd done that this afternoon, which was why she happened to be leaving the office later than usual.

She usually tried to get out of here while the streets were still crowded from building front to curb with hundreds and thousands of nine-to-fivers hustling to get where they wanted to go at the end of the workday. She'd slide right into that press of souls who paid little or no attention to her though she kept a close eye on them. She also quit work at a different time each day. A predictable routine can be the downfall of anyone trying to avoid discovery. Even making allowance for varying her routine, tonight she was leaving the office later than she would have preferred.

The twenty-eighth floor was deserted with no light shining from any of the doorways. The shadowed cavern of the long, narrow corridor suddenly reminded her of a tomb. The minute she heard herself having that thought, she knew she was spooked. She got that way at times. It came with the territory of being constantly watchful. She always turned out to have spooked herself over nothing. She reminded herself of that now as she hurried toward the elevators. Still, the skin on the back of her neck felt as if it might be trying to shrink off her spine.

She poked the elevator button several times in rapid succession though she knew that wouldn't make it arrive any faster. She wanted to get out of this building, which was putting her more in mind of a mausoleum by the minute. The clunk of the elevator landing at her floor and the doors opening were music to her ears. She was also relieved to find the car occupied until it occurred to her that she'd never seen this guy around here before. She was inside by then with her finger pressing the door-close button. She might be able to switch to the door-open button and make a dash for it back onto twenty-eight, but what then? If this was a bad guy, he could easily follow her out into the deserted hallway, and she'd be on her own with him again. The lobby button was already lit, and the door was closing. She told herself he was probably okay and did her best to relax.

She could feel the eyes of the car's other occupant watching her. Reaching into her coat pocket, she gripped the thin, black canister of pepper spray she kept there. She wished it were Mace instead, but that was illegal in New York State. There were places to get it, but she was as leery of getting into trouble with the police and having the past catch up with her that way as she was of the bad guys who might be after her. She restrained herself from punching the lobby button again and gripped the metal canister so hard she was in danger of peppering her pocket lining.

The elevator reached the lobby level at last, without stopping for a single additional passenger. Delia really was getting out of here late tonight. In the lobby, the guard usually on duty was nowhere to be seen. Delia took a right toward the Rockefeller Plaza end of the building. She fully expected her elevator companion to be hot on her heels, but when she glanced behind her she saw him headed in the opposite direction toward the Sixth Avenue exit. He was also glancing back at her with a very wary expression on his face. She understood then what must have happened. He'd been watching her jumpy performance in the elevator so closely because he thought he might be trapped in there with a nut case who could leap on him at any moment. Delia almost laughed out loud at how close she'd come to staining his well-tailored topcoat with a liberal dose of pepper spray.

Still, she kept herself alert. She took a few deep breaths to make sure she was calm, as well, as she passed through the revolving doors out of 30 Rock Center and into the street. The spectacle of the Plaza Christmas tree took her by surprise as always, towering into the sky just across from the entrance to her office building. What looked like a million colored lights sparkled from the branches of the majestic pine that was one of the city's most popular yuletide attractions. Delia permitted herself a moment of holiday heart-swell before returning full attention to her immediate sur-roundings.

That's when she saw him. She was checking window reflections, as was her habit, pretending to examine the merchandise while she scanned the crowd behind her for exactly what she'd just spotted—a person whose gen-eral demeanor didn't quite fit the profile of a random face in the crowd. He was a tall man and big enough to give her considerable trouble in a confrontation. He was also just a bit too watchful, especially in her direction. Delia's years in hiding, along with her experience in the protection business, had given her an extra keen sense for detecting such behavior. That detection apparatus was out of tune back in the elevator. She'd been spooked then, and that could knock everything out of kilter. She wasn't spooked now. She was almost a hun-dred percent certain that this man was on her tail. Still, she didn't run away or even pick up speed. She stead-ied her pace into her usual gait. The man might have followed her on other occasions. If that was the case and if he was good at the shadowing game, he'd be likely to notice any unusual behavior on her part, such as taking off at a gallop down the street.

The holiday crowd was too dense here to make much progress anyway, even at a run. Tourists lined the opposite sidewalk several deep and spilled over the curb into the street to gape up at the tree. Delia had turned right out of 30 Rock Center toward Forty-ninth Street. She continued in that direction to the corner then turned onto Forty-ninth and crossed the road pavement in the direction of Fifth Avenue. She glanced back over her shoulder as she crossed. The tall man was still following. She returned her attention to looking for an opportunity, whatever it might be, to get away from him. A crowd lined this side of the Plaza, as well, leaning toward the brass rail to watch the ice skaters spin around Rockefeller Center Rink beneath the imposing tree. Bright strains of holiday music piped from speakers camouflaged by decorative evergreens. Excitement charged the air. Delia kept herself steely calm by contrast as she searched for an escape route.

She eased her black wool beret out of her left coat pocket while her other hand once again gripped the pepper canister on the right. She generally kept her hair a dark brownish, innocuous shade, only faintly auburn, but the hairdresser had missed that mark this time. The result was more conspicuously coppery than she'd intended and far easier to pick out in a crowd than Delia's usual mousey dark brown would have been. She needed a chance to be out of her pursuer's range of vision long enough to make her first move at disappearing while she was still right in front of him. She spotted that chance halfway down the block.

A glass kiosk framed in polished brass marked the street level access to the lower concourse of Rockefeller Plaza. Too many people were already trying to squeeze into the small, domed enclosure. Delia wedged in among them, shoving herself into the center of the pack. Despite her "Excuse me's," there were grumblings and remarks about rude New Yorkers from every side. She concentrated on wriggling out of her coat with one hand while jamming her beret on her head and stuffing her hair under it with the other. The glass-and-brass elevator car purred to a stop three people in front of her. The elevator door, which constituted the inside wall of the kiosk, eased open and the press of bodies tumbled through, carrying Delia with it.

Her maneuverings with her coat and hat had further irritated her fellow passengers. She took a couple of elbows to the ribs in response, but she didn't care. She was inside the elevator and headed downward, leaving the street and her human shadow behind. She'd caught sight of him hurrying past as she jammed herself into the kiosk elevator. He was peering ahead into the street crowd at the time. That single glimpse of his exasperated expression convinced Delia she'd been right. He was searching the street for her.

The elevator door opened at the lower level, and Delia spilled out along with the crowd. She ignored their parting accusatory glances, too relieved to be bothered by a bit of public embarrassment. The sparkling white marble concourse seemed too pristine a place for anything very horrible to happen. That lightened her state of mind only a little and not enough to keep her from coming to the obvious and unavoidable conclusion. She needed help, and it had to be somebody good. It also had to be somebody she didn't usually employ at PEI.

She needed to keep this personal situation as separate from her work life as possible. The elevator had deposited her only a few feet from the entrance to the Sea Grill Restaurant. She walked to the doorway and glanced in the direction of the bar. She'd be able to sit down there and think for a moment, though she already had an answer to her dilemma in mind.

She'd kept track of Nick Avery through the bodyguard network ever since she started PEI, but she'd never hired him. That would have been too risky, both to her hidden identity and to her determination to avoid personal involvements. She'd never completely abandoned the fantasy of him that kept her company in her loneliest moments. She'd specifically kept track of when he was here in New York, where he generally spent any time he might have between jobs. She even knew where he stayed when he was in town, at an out-of-the-way hotel in Soho. She'd imagined going there many times, just to catch a glimpse of him, but she never had. He was in Manhattan now. She rummaged in her coat pocket, under the canister of pepper spray, for the quarters she kept there. She picked up a coin then dropped it again. She couldn't call Nick. It was too risky. Still, as she declined the steward's offer to take her coat and headed past the gleaming tables and away from the glass wall onto the white marble concourse, Delia's heart was beating very hard with what felt like anticipation.

Chapter Three

Nick Avery had been living in hotels so long they'd begun to feel like home to him, or as much like home as he cared to deal with. He'd have an assignment here, an assignment there all over the country. He told himself it wasn't practical to set up a base residence he'd hardly ever be in. Actually, he liked living this way, most of the time. He thought of himself as in tune with one of the major lessons he'd learned about living in general: nothing lasts very long and you're smart to have a bag half packed and ready for takeoff the minute things fall through. He'd had that bag in his closet for the past five years.

He was saving up a nest egg, too, though he hadn't yet decided exactly what for. The great escape maybe. Someday he'd cut loose from even the spindly roots he had now and kick back someplace where it was warm forever and he didn't speak the language. That way he wouldn't be tempted to tell any of the too many secrets he knew about too many people. Or, maybe what he'd been building up was a cushion thick enough to keep from mangling any limbs when everything finally fell through for good and he came plummeting down. He figured it was mostly the cushion he had in mind. Besides, he was one hundred percent Scot. He carried caution in his bones.

When Nick was in Manhattan, he stayed at the Tivoli Hotel on Mercer Street in Soho. He preferred to go back to the same place in each city he frequented. This small illusion of belonging somewhere saved him from having to think of himself as totally on the drift. He usually chose a hotel like this one, with character and plenty of street life around the neighborhood. Maybe the Tivoli was his version of a hometown. This would be the second Christmas in a row he'd spent here. Last year there'd been a card slipped under his door on Christmas Eve with a peace dove on the front and "Happy Holidays from the Management" printed in red foil letters on the inside. All of the staff had signed, even the day maids. A couple of them wrote brief, semipersonal messages along with their names. Mindy, the night clerk, wrote something more personal than semi, but he'd ignored it. He didn't intend to mess up the comfortable thing he had going here by getting involved with somebody on staff. He might still have that card tucked into one of the handy, pack rat pockets of his bag in the closet. Something kept him from throwing it out. In general, however, his attitude was that holidays didn't have much to do with him. They were about family, and he didn't really have one.

Thinking about that now turned Nick restless. He hopped up off the bed, which was the only really comfortable seat in the room, and paced to the window. He was on the front side of the hotel with brick buildings across the narrow street and people bustling back and forth on the sidewalk below. Many of them were loaded down with packages, probably from the fancy shops over on West Broadway. He could see the tinseled paper twinkle in the streetlights even from up here. He paced back to the bed but didn't sit down. Holidays! There was no getting away from them.

The television set murmured and flickered from the corner of the room. He hadn't been watching, only using it for background noise. The picture switched from some silly sitcom to a commercial of a guy in a Santa Claus hat in front of a bank of CD players, then cellular phones, then TV sets. Nick grabbed the remote from the bedside table and gave the Off button a savage punch. He needed a new assignment. He needed to get out of this room. He'd go to a movie. He was only a few blocks from the Angelika. That was one place he could count on them not to be playing *It's A Wonderful Life.* Nick grabbed his brown suede jacket from the chair near the window and was almost to the door when the phone rang. He hesitated. He really didn't want to talk to anybody. Then he remembered that nobody ever called him here except about a job. He'd just been thinking he needed a job. He picked up the phone.

"Avery, here."

Nobody answered, but he could hear breathing. "This is Nick Avery. Can I help you?"

"I hope so."

The voice on the other end of the line was calm but pitched unnaturally low, almost to a whisper, as if she didn't want anybody around her to hear. Nick recognized the sound of someone who might be in trouble.

"Who is this?"

It occurred to Nick that calls from possible customers went to his service first. Then they called him to make sure he wanted to respond. Where did this woman get his direct number? How did she know he was in town anyway?

"This is Delia Marie Barry. I'm with Protective Enterprises, Inc.," she said.

That answered Nick's immediate questions. He'd instructed his service to give his direct number to any of the bodyguard services that might want to hire him. The surprise was that this was the first time PEI had called. He was one of the top names in the bodyguard game, even if he did say so himself. Still, PEI seemed to avoid him like the plague. He'd wondered who at Delia Barry's office had tossed in the blackball on Nick Avery. Now they were calling at last, probably because it was the holidays and everybody wanted vacation time so the great PEI was in a bind for talent.

Nick was considering whether or not to blow them off as he said, "What can I do for you?"

DELIA WENT INTO the Sea Grill's ladies' room as soon as she got off the pay phone outside of it. She needed to calm herself. She hadn't known his voice would have such an effect on her. "Avery, here." It was an abrupt sort of greeting in the first place, but she would have been startled by anything he said. She was that unprepared. She'd fantasized about calling him many times, just as she had about going to his hotel. She would plan out what she had to say, like a script for a scene, so she wouldn't get on the phone and be the way she was a few minutes ago—stunned and confused. She'd never actually made any of those fantasy calls. Unfortunately, tonight she had. Now she could hardly remember what she'd said. Had it been something stupid? She couldn't be sure.

She'd hoped to be alone in the ladies' room. Unfortunately, she'd forgotten about the presence of a washroom attendant. The one on duty that evening was a kindly looking woman in an extremely clean, white ruffled apron. She smiled as she held out a hand towel made of paper so fine it could pass for cloth. Delia took the towel and did her best to return the smile, though she was about ready to jump out of her skin with anxiety. She stared into the mirror but didn't really see herself. She had to get in control and stay that way. She turned on the sink tap and dampened the paper towel with warm water then touched it to her throat where she could feel the tightness intensifying and her pulse working. The attendant walked away as if she were busy with other things rather than trying to avoid staring at Delia in her obviously troubled state.

This day had turned out badly enough already, with Delia finding herself under surveillance and all the terrifying possibilities that brought to mind. As if all of that wasn't enough to drive her crazy, she'd called Nick Avery. She should have stopped to think. She might have decided against it. Too late for that now. He was on his way here. And she'd given him her name.

Delia's first urge was to dry her hands, leave the attendant a tip and make a run for it, back through the restaurant to the concourse and out the door before Nick got here. There were lots of exits from Rockefeller Plaza. Whoever was following her couldn't be at all of them, unless he wasn't alone. Delia found it hard to believe there was a phalanx of operatives out there lying in wait for Delia Marie Barry née Rebecca Radley Lester. Still, she'd be taking a chance at least by her choice of exits, like Russian roulette with escape routes.

She tried to calculate what would be the best, as in safest, alternative, but her mind refused to cooperate. All she could think about was how Nick's voice on the phone thrilled through her like a sudden shattering of glass. She reminded herself that she was in trouble. She needed help. She needed protection. She needed a bodyguard, and Nick best suited those needs at the moment. That consideration had to remain foremost in her mind. Every ounce of common sense she possessed told her this was true. She must go through with meeting him tonight. She'd do her best to keep him from recognizing her. She'd already invented a cover story to go with her much altered appearance. She really did look entirely different from five years ago. Men tended to be easily fooled by superficials like hair color and style, makeup, clothing type. She'd changed all of that dramatically. Would he recognize her voice the way she'd recognized his—immediately? Had they really talked all that much five years ago? She'd had a smart-aleck tone back then, anyway.

Delia balled the paper towel up tight and pushed it through the waste chute door. She absolutely could not let herself think about the past. If she did, she'd come undone for sure. She had an important acting job ahead of her tonight. She couldn't afford to be undone. The acting part was what would save her. She'd be playing Delia Marie Barry, a woman who hadn't yet been born five years ago.

She rummaged in her bag for a dollar and put it in the china tip plate. The attendant thanked her, and Delia smiled back, much more broadly than before. She was getting into character, a character she was about to play to the hilt.

Chapter Four

By the time Nick arrived, Delia had her story down pat. She'd even taken off her gold ring, the one with the circle of aspen leaves her mother had given her. There was little chance Nick had ever seen it, but she slipped it off anyway. Now she was ready for him—or so she thought, until she saw him. Suddenly, she could barely breathe much less think.

He was just as she remembered, strong-boned in the face, tall in the body. Yet he was different. For one thing, his eyes had lost their arrogance. They were cool but not so challenging. His features had a haggard edge she was certain hadn't been there before, as if the time since might not have been easy for him. His handsomeness had been almost too smooth five years ago. This new, life-marred face might be less picture perfect, but she found it even more affecting than she had the last time she'd seen him.

The last time she'd seen him was in her fantasies— He was halfway across the restaurant, striding toward the bar in a suede jacket and dark slacks, but she was seeing his long, naked flank on the bed beside her. The sheen of his skin in the moonlight from a window drew her fingers to slide along the contour of him, over the jut of his hipbone where she could feel the skeleton beneath the skin and slip her thumb into the shadowed hollow below the bone. She ran the flat of her palm across his thigh to that curious juncture where smooth flesh became a dark pelt of hair, wiry yet soft to her touch. Her movements were hypnotic, in sync with her entrancement. Such a sweet and tender moment with so few to match it, at least in her real life.

Delia felt the moistness in her eyes and ducked her head while she blinked it back. When she looked up again, he was at the end of the bar. His eyes met hers, and she felt the breath catch in her throat. Then his glance moved on. A few seconds passed before her mind could truly register what had happened. He didn't recognize her. The disappointment of that struck her like a blow, all the harder because she hadn't expected to be disappointed by the achievement of her goal. Her disguise had worked. She didn't look anything like she had back in Colorado. Or... Another possibility hit her with even more impact. He'd meant so much to her five years ago she'd never imagined that, just maybe, she hadn't been particularly important to him at all.

He had returned his glance to the bar, and he'd begun to walk toward her. She had to get a grip on her emotions. She was generally so in control. Yet right now she felt herself literally carried away on a wave of memory and sensation stronger than any control. She couldn't let that happen. She held her breath for a moment and concentrated on pulling her straying emotions back within reach. She must keep her purpose in mind. She could sort out the rest of it later. She let her breath out in a gush then raised her hand to signal Nick toward her.

He quickened his pace down the bar. "Delia Barry?"

"Yes," she said and extended her hand. "You must be Nick Avery."

She made her voice confident and straightforward, totally unlike the bantering sarcastic tone of her younger, more mixed-up years. She was in charge of herself again. When he took her hand, she was even ready for the shock of touching him, as ready as she could be. She looked directly into his eyes and steeled herself against the flutter inside that threatened to undo her calm exterior. He held her gaze a moment longer than expected. He let go of her hand then and took the stool next to hers. Delia felt the relief of no longer touching him and the desire to grab his hand again at the same instant.

"You said on the phone that this was an urgent case," he began.

"Yes, it is." She was surprised to hear her voice ring out, still clear and confident.

"Who's the client?"

"I am."

He'd lifted his hand in a casual motion to get the bartender's attention. Slowly, he put his hand down and turned toward Delia. His scrutiny was even more intense than it had been a moment ago. She took a deep breath and willed herself to suppress the blaze his eyes threatened to raise on her cheeks.

"A personal situation has come up for me," she said before he could question further.

"What kind of situation?"

The bartender had arrived. Delia waited while Nick ordered a beer. Her mineral water with a slice of lime sat untouched on the bar, the ice melting in the tall glass. Nick turned toward her.

"An old boyfriend," she said, just as she'd planned. "He's been stalking me. He followed me from the office tonight. I came in here to lose him."

"An old boyfriend," Nick repeated. He looked her up and down quickly as if confirming for himself whether or not she might be stalking material. "How long has he been after you?"

"A few weeks now." She turned away from Nick and stared into her mineral water. It was easier to lie when she wasn't looking at him. "He's been more persistent lately."

"Has he threatened you with anything specific?"

Delia had anticipated his questions, and her answers were ready. Bodyguarding was her business, too. She knew the routine.

"He doesn't need to make overt threats. I know what he's capable of."

Keep it simple, she'd counseled herself in planning her approach to this conversation. There are fewer details to remember that way.

"You were with him a long time?"

"Long enough."

"How long would that be?"

"Several months."

"I see."

Delia could tell from the timbre of his voice that he was inquiring about her supposed sexual relationship with this fictitious boyfriend. She could also tell that Nick was just a bit uneasy with discussing the subject. She wondered why. He didn't seem like the prim, old-fashioned type.

"If you were with him for that long, didn't you pick up on these . . . tendencies of his?"

She could hear an edge of disapproval in Nick's tone. That might be good for keeping him at the distance needed for making sure he didn't recognize her. She resisted the impulse to curry his favor.

"Maybe I should have suspected, but I didn't. He seemed like a regular guy until I decided not to see him anymore."

Nick's beer had arrived. He took a long sip before responding. "What made you decide that?"

Did she hear a hint of something more than professional interest in that question? If so, what was the reason for it?

"We turned out not to have as much in common as I'd thought. I couldn't see the point in continuing."

"So you dropped the guy?" Disapproval again.

"Something like that."

"And that drove him crazy?"

More disapproval. The hint of personal interest was gone. Delia didn't answer.

"I'd have thought that somebody in your line of work would know how dangerous it is to take up with just anyone, especially in this town," he said.

Delia was beginning to get exasperated with his judgments. She reminded herself that this was only playacting on her part. She had to stick to the script. Still, she couldn't help trying to recall if he'd had this rigid side to his personality five years ago.

"He wasn't 'just anybody,'" she said. "We were introduced by a mutual acquaintance."

Nick took another sip of beer and shook his head, as if she hadn't convinced him that her behavior was anything but foolish and irresponsible.

"Do you have a picture of him?"

She was ready for that question, too. "I only had one, and I got rid of it after we stopped seeing each other."

"Just like you got rid of him?"

Delia was becoming more and more bothered by his tone. Who was he to put her down this way? She had to remind herself yet again that this was a charade and she shouldn't be reacting as if it were real.

"His name is Clyde Benno. He lives on Long Island," she said, supplying the details she'd concocted. "I can write out a description of him, but you don't have to hunt him down. I would only be hiring you to keep me safe."

He looked her over again, as if he might be judging whether or not she was deserving of that safety.

"Will you take the assignment?" she asked, forcing herself to keep from showing her irritation with him.

Nick pushed his beer glass away from him a few inches across the bar. "Sure," he said. "Why not? I've got nothing else going right now. I could use the gig."

Delia stifled the urge to upend the glass over his head and watch the foamy liquid wash the smug expression from his face.

"Good," she said.

"When do I start?"

"You've already started."

Delia motioned for the bartender to bring the check.

"I'll get that," Nick said.

"No, you won't," she responded more quickly than was probably cool to do, but she felt she had to establish the ground rules between them right off. "You're working for me. I pay the bills."

"Yes, ma'am," Nick said with exaggerated deference.

The ground rules had been established, but Delia would say they were getting off to anything but a good start.

NICK COULD HARDLY believe the way she ticked him off. He almost turned her down for the job, but this was his intro to PEI. He'd been hoping to crack that particular professional nut for a long time now. If that meant putting up with Delia Marie Barry, he could handle it. This should be a test all the same, of how much he could take without blowing his top. He didn't let himself get too far out on the anger scale very often. Still, he had his limit like any man, and something told him she was going to press him up against that limit eventually.

Speaking of pressing up against something, she was one sexy woman. Tall, and rounded in the right places under that uptight suit she had on. Good legs, too, what he could see of them with her skirt down to her knees. He liked short hemlines himself, but he could tell she was all business. No thighs to be peered at for Delia. On the other hand, she must have shown some thigh and maybe more to this poor guy who was on her tail. Nick told himself he shouldn't be thinking of a stalker as a poor guy, and ordinarily he never would. Nick had to keep straight about which side he was on here. Still, he couldn't help feeling a twinge of sympathy. He didn't like women who got a guy turned on to them then took a walk, as if nobody's feelings mattered but their own. He didn't care for men who did that to women, either. Nick knew what it felt like to be out in the cold.

Maybe that's what had his back up about Delia. She was one of those women who changed her mind and gave some poor sap the brush-off. He wondered if she dropped out of this guy's life with no warning. That's how it had happened to Nick. He'd done his best to keep from tumbling for Rebecca Lester in the first place, but every time he'd turn around there she was in his face till he couldn't think anymore, unless he was thinking about her. Then she was gone, with a murder rap hanging over her and him left on the hot seat to answer the hard questions. He didn't think she'd done it, but sometimes he wished he could believe she had. It would be easier to consign her to the villain column. That would put her beyond the pale even for his imagination. He'd been a cop once, back before Rebecca's father had lured him into this business. A clean cop didn't get mixed up with a killer unless the cop was pretty mixed up himself. Nick had been a clean cop, and now he was a clean ex-cop.

It still bothered him to remember how she hadn't trusted him enough to let him help her. She'd taken off without so much as a word, which made her look guilty as hell. They'd traced her through the flight she took to Chicago, but couldn't turn her up after that. They'd scoured the club scene and anywhere else somebody like her might have ended up in the Midwest, but nothing shook out. She could have taken a Greyhound bus anywhere, with no way to follow that trail. He figured Canada was her best bet, maybe Europe from there. She had a stash to bankroll herself, nobody knew how much, but enough to get her hidden where she wasn't likely to surface again. Now, even after five years, she was still under his skin like a piece of thorn he'd never been able to work out all the way.

Meanwhile, he and Delia had cabbed it downtown from Rockefeller Center to where she lived across from Gramercy Park. He wanted to check her security system. As it turned out, she'd taken a lot of precautions, especially for a small apartment. She'd installed two tamper-resistant locks on the door to be opened from the outside and a police lock inside. Her windows were security gated, as well.

"I spend so much time talking to people who fear for their lives, some of it must have rubbed off on me," she said, shrugging almost sheepishly.

Nick was surprised to see a flash of something endearing in the way she did that.

"Go ahead with whatever you'd normally be doing now," he said. "I want to case the place one more time on my own."

"Well." She hesitated. "Normally, I take a shower when I get home."

"Take a shower then."

She looked at him with obvious suspicion in her eyes.

"I promise not to case the bathroom while you're in there," he said.

"Okay," she said, and nodded.

The sheepishness hadn't entirely left her. He wondered why she was looking more attractive to him all of a sudden. She'd been pretty all along, no getting around that, but he didn't usually go for just looks. He had to find more than that in a woman, coming from inside instead of just what could be seen on the outside. Heart was what he called it. Even when he thought it was there he could be fooled, like with Rebecca back in Colorado. She'd been all toughness on the exterior, but he would have sworn she was hiding a tender self underneath. When she took off the way she did, he suspected he'd been wrong about her and she was as hard inside as out. The same could be true of Ms. Barry. She came across as cactus on the outside. She just might be cactus through and through.

She'd gone on into the bedroom and the bathroom past that. He could hear the water running already. He'd take a closer look at the rest of the apartment now, in more detail than it was sometimes comfortable to do with the client watching. They got nervous about letting him inside their private worlds, and he understood why. He could learn a lot of things about a person just by checking out their belongings. He wondered what he'd learn about her.

First of all, this room was softer than he'd expected of her. The walls were painted a creamy off-white. Medium-level light from a number of table lamps brought out the warm tones in the muted rose and dusty blue of the thick cushioned couch and chair. He would have pegged her for a high-tech type, but there wasn't a hint of that anywhere here. He was drawn to a claw-footed table that looked like it belonged in somebody's grandmother's house. The oval oak top was crowded with photographs in antique frames. He figured they must be pictures of her family—dark hair like hers, but solid salt-of-the-earth faces. She must be the beauty of the Barry clan.

The deep windowsill near the table was fitted with a tapestry cushion seat. Nick sat down there and looked out. The park was across the street, with a gate locked to anyone but neighborhood residents. He wondered if she had a key. He examined the window guards—accordion design, installed inside the window, fire department standard approved. Good for urban situations. The streetlight across the way glinted on the exterior windowsill. He put his face next to the glass to examine the source of that reflection. Grease—she'd covered the entire surface of the outside sill with grease.

He'd heard of doing that to keep an intruder from getting either a foot or handhold. She appeared to have regreased the surface regularly, too, because there were no gaps or smudges from wear or weather. She must really be scared of this guy who was following her. Nick wondered if she could be exaggerating. Or was the danger as marked as she obviously believed? His job was to assume the latter. From that perspective, he approved of the greased windowsills and any other extraordinary precautions she might take.

Nick sensed more than heard a movement behind him. Guarding people for ten years had made him so finely tuned to his environment that sometimes he wished he could turn off his hyperawareness and be half here, half not here like everybody else. He snapped his head around to establish the validity of his sensation, and there she was. She was standing in the doorway of the bedroom. She hadn't put on something provocative, as she might have if she were coming on to him, but she was provocative all the same. Her hair was damp, combed back off her face and close to the scalp. Her face was most pointedly visible that way. He hadn't noticed how big her eyes were before, or how clear and pale her skin was. She wasn't wearing makeup, and she didn't need any. The shower had brought out a dewy flush on her cheeks. Nick felt an urge to reach out and touch the softness he could see there. He clenched his hand into a fist instead as he rose from the window seat.

"You greased the sill," he said. He motioned awkwardly toward the window. He could hear just as much awkwardness in the way his voice rasped over his words. He cleared his throat. "I hope you did that in all the rooms."

He knew how far that statement was from what was suddenly in his mind to say to her. He also knew that he'd been without a woman for a very long time, and when he did get involved with one again it definitely should not be her.

DELIA COULD HARDLY believe how fast Nick hotfooted it out of her apartment after she finished her shower. She also could hardly believe how much she hated to see him go. She plopped down on the couch and leaned back against the cushions, unconcerned about the mark her damp hair was making there. She was very tired all of a sudden. Her limbs ached as if she'd been running hard into a gale-force wind till she was too exhausted to go on. Her feelings about Nick seemed to have that effect on her.

She'd asked for this. She'd fantasized her reunion with him a thousand times before tonight, and always there was upheaval involved. She was too realistic a person to expect otherwise. It was one thing, however, to anticipate an imagined experience and quite another to find herself smack in the middle of the real-life version.

Of course, she could always call and leave a message with his exchange saying she'd changed her mind and didn't think they could work together because the chemistry was wrong. That certainly rang true. She could get any number of other very competent pros to bodyguard for her. She'd have fewer hassles to put up with that way for sure. Delia actually picked up the cordless phone from her coffee table. She stared at the buttons as if trying to remember what they were for. Then she lay the phone down on her lap where she'd tucked her robe around her legs to keep warm. She stared at the ceiling with her head still at the center of the damp mark, like a halo of shadow on the couch cushion.

Chapter Five

By morning, Delia had reconciled herself to keeping Nick around, for practical safety reasons if nothing else. He picked her up at her apartment in the morning as they'd planned before he left last night. He insisted they take a cab uptown. He said she shouldn't risk the subway for the time being. She reluctantly agreed, though she hated to change her life for the sake of whoever was after her. He'd have won somehow then, even if he didn't manage to catch her and do something to her. She shuddered at the thought.

"Are you cold?" Nick asked.

They were in her office where she'd been trying all morning to get some work done.

"No," she said, then thought better of it. "Actually, I think I might have picked up a chill."

Nick looked concerned. "Stress can make you sick. That happens a lot in these situations."

"Is that right?" He didn't know the half of it.

"You have to keep healthy."

"Why? In case I need my strength to fight off an attacker?" Or to fight off my feelings for you? she thought.

"Let's hope it doesn't come to that."

He'd been checking windows and sweeping the place for listening devices for hours. Anybody could buy surveillance equipment now, especially in this city. Delia stayed in the outer office to maintain the illusion that she was only the office manager here. Lily Tubman, Delia's sometime clerical worker, wasn't in today. Delia hired her on a temporary basis to prevent her from knowing too much about the internal operations of the business. She'd work at PEI for a few months, then Delia would send her back to the temp agency saying she wasn't needed anymore. Delia had gone through a few dozen office workers in five years that way, and several agencies, too. The transitions were more and more unsettling each time they happened. Delia especially didn't want to lose Lily. She was a good worker, and Delia liked her personally. Still, maintaining cover had to come first.

Speaking of cover, she'd spent the first two hours of her workday checking the office for anything that might give Nick even the smallest clue to her true identity. She used the excuse of cleaning up for the holidays. Nick appeared to take very little notice of what she was doing, anyway. His attention was focused on making the place as secure as possible. Meanwhile, she didn't find anything that needed hiding. She'd eradicated all trace of Becky Lester long ago. Still, Delia found the effort tiring, or maybe she hadn't rested up enough from last night's exhaustion. She hadn't slept well, either. Aside from her maddeningly conflicted feelings about Nick, she was very aware of being targeted. That's what being followed really meant. She was the object of somebody's special scrutiny. She had no idea who that somebody might be and could only guess at their motive. The strain of trying to sort out the particulars and decide how to respond to them was enough to knock the energy out of anyone.

"I think I'm going to close up for the afternoon," she said, intending to go home and rest.

"Can you do that?"

Delia almost said, "Why not?" Then she remembered her charade, the deception that was her life.

"I just have to make a couple of calls and put a message on the phone service. We have an assistant office manager who fills in when I need her. This is a slow week for us anyway with Christmas coming. Besides, I hardly ever take time off so nobody should begrudge my doing it today."

She realized she was explaining too much and stopped talking. She didn't tell him that, in fact, she hadn't taken a single vacation or sick day in five years. That would sound too weird for somebody in a mere lower middle management job. Again, she had to keep her cover in mind at all times.

They left the office and found a taxi. Traffic was heavy on the way downtown.

"We'll get out here," she said to the cabdriver when they were within walking distance of Gramercy Park.

She thrust the fare through the opening in the safety slide between the front and back seat before Nick could protest.

"We were better off in the car than out here on the street," he said as he hurried up onto the curb after her. "And wait for me. Don't go running off on your own. You ought to have this bodyguard routine down pat by now."

"For other people, not for me."

The weather had turned cold overnight and was even colder now than when they'd been out in it that morning. Delia pulled her coat collar up around her face. She thought about putting on her hat, but she was actually enjoying the chill in the air as it revived her from her daylong torpor.

"You'd be less visible in that beret you had on last night," he said as if he might have read her thoughts. "Your hair makes you stand out too much."

The winter sun was bright enough this afternoon to shine down past the buildings onto East Twenty-first Street. She imagined it must be setting her reddish tresses aglow.

"I like to feel the wind," she said.

He'd been so preoccupied with watching the street in all directions ever since they left the cab that she was surprised he'd had the opportunity to notice her hair.

"You aren't going to make my job easy for me, are you?"

"You should keep me safe," she said, "but I still want to have a life."

"Sometimes those two don't come in the same package."

Mention of packages turned her attention to the shopping bags so many people were carrying as they hurried past. Delia hadn't thought about the holidays or how much she enjoyed them since she'd first spotted that man behind her yesterday. She needed something to get her out of this fearful, downcast state of mind. She broke into the chorus of a Christmas song.

She had a fairly pleasant singing voice, trained in the high school chorus and, when her father was alive, the church choir. Nonetheless, Nick looked at her as if she'd made the most outlandish sound he'd ever heard. He was still looking at her that way when she spotted the tree vendor across the street on the edge of the park and took off toward him.

"I told you to stick with me," said Nick as he caught up to her, his breath making puffs of white when he spoke.

"Sorry," she said. "I saw the trees and forgot."

The smell of evergreen was so pungent with memories that Delia was afraid she'd start weeping on the spot.

"Blue spruce," she said to get herself under control. "Blue spruce is my favorite."

The vendor was already pulling bundled evergreens out of the pile he'd leaned against a black iron fence. "How tall you want it?" he asked.

Delia couldn't think for a moment. She was too overcome by the heady scent of pine and the sound of carols tinkling from a portable tape player the man had set up on a crate among his wares.

"How tall do you think?" she asked Nick.

He was busy scanning the street with a disgruntled expression on his face. "Six feet," he said without looking at her.

"That's pretty big," she said.

"I hate those dinky little things that sit on a table. You might as well not bother with a tree at all if you're going to have one of them."

Delia gave Nick a quizzical look. He almost sounded like he was getting some holiday spirit. More likely he was going along with her to move her through the tree purchase as rapidly as possible.

"You'll have to carry it." Delia motioned toward the tree the vendor had just pulled out of the stack. "I'll take that one."

She barely had time to get the cash out of her purse when Nick grabbed the tree.

"Help me hoist this onto my shoulder," he said to the man.

Nick bent his knees but kept his back straight to take the weight of the tree. He grasped it around the thickest width with his left arm.

"You gotta hold onta it wit' both hands," the vendor said.

Nick maintained his one-handed grip. Delia understood why. He had to keep his right-side, weapon hand free.

"I'll help," she said as she pressed the bills on the vendor.

"Then get in front of me," Nick said. "Where I can see you."

She nodded and hurried to the top end of the tree, which had begun to wobble in Nick's precarious grasp. She latched on and called, "Ready," over her shoulder.

They began walking toward the next corner. "We'll go around the park to my place," she said.

"This has to be the most foolish thing anybody ever asked me to do on a job," Nick grumbled.

Even more foolish were Delia's first attempts to match his gait. The tree tottered from side to side even though, unlike Nick, she was holding it with both hands.

"Take shorter strides," she called over her shoulder again. "You're about to run me down."

"I want to get off this street and under cover," he growled. Still, he slowed his pace. "What if that guy who's stalking you catches us out here in the open wrestling with this damned tree?"

The image of Nick taking off after a desperado with the blue spruce in tow made Delia want to laugh. She swallowed the impulse and hurried along as he directed. She knew it was tension and tiredness rather than true merriment that she was feeling. All the same, she had to bite back another urge to giggle.

NICK COULDN'T help smiling at himself. Here he was hauling a gigantic Christmas tree up the front steps to this woman's apartment house and getting paid for his time while doing it. He wouldn't find this duty listed in the bodyguard's manual, even if there'd been such a publication. He had to smile at her, too, being followed all over town by some nut and having the heart to think about putting up a Christmas tree anyway. Too bad Nick wasn't free to think like that himself. He was on the job.

He'd propped the tree against the outside stair rail and entered the downstairs lobby ahead of Delia to make certain the area was clear. He did the same with each staircase and landing. Delia's apartment was on the third floor. He left her at the top of the last stairway with the tree angled against the wall in a corner while he checked the hallway leading to her door. That's when he knew something was wrong. He signaled Delia to come ahead and join him. What he'd seen indicated that she'd be better off inside the apartment.

"What about the tree?" she called from the stairway.

Nick put his finger to his lips to caution silence. He waved his arms back and forth, crossing them in front of him—meaning to nix the tree for now—then beckoned her to come, all with what he hoped was an expression of urgency on his face. She moved down the landing toward him as he pulled his gun from the back of his waistband out of her line of vision. With his empty hand he gestured for her to get away from the banister and keep herself against the wall. She did that without hesitation. This was the first time he'd seen her cooperate so readily. One look at her face told him why. Her green eyes were wide with fear.

She'd inched along the wall till she was next to him. He could hear her gasping breath. He had the urge to reassure her, but he knew he mustn't. The alertness her fear brought with it could keep her ready to react quickly. Meanwhile he saw the questions in her eyes. He made the silence motion with his finger to his lips again. She mouthed, "What's going on?" He shook his head in response, to signal that he couldn't answer her now. He motioned downward then, for her to crouch lower against the wall. "Stay here," he mouthed, and she nodded.

Nick moved low and fast along the wall to the next stairway. He held his gun gripped in both hands and pointed upward directly in front of his face. He hesitated a moment, then leapt around the corner into a crouch at the bottom of the stairwell with his gun barrel aimed at what was, thank God, empty space. He maintained the crouch and climbed several steps with his back brushing the stairwell wall and his gun pointed at the fourth-floor landing above. Nothing up there, either. The inside of the building looked secure.

He moved quickly back down to the third floor and along the wall to Delia's door. Her eyes were even wider now and focused on his gun as if stuck there. Her mouth had dropped open. He already had his free hand in his jeans pocket, clutching the three front door keys on a ring that she'd given him last night. He pulled out the keys and turned one in the main lock, a second in the backup lock, then a third in the police lock. He motioned for her to stay where she was till he went inside. His guess was the intruder hadn't gotten in here, but it would be best to double-check before bringing Delia along. Nick made a circuit of the living room, bedroom and bath with his firearm preceding him into each space. All was clear.

He went back to the apartment door.

"You can come in now," he said.

She scurried through the doorway. He took one last visual sweep up and down the hall. The bundled evergreen was still propped in the corner at the top of the stairway from the second floor. He'd go back and get it later, after he made certain Delia was okay. He shut the apartment door.

"Be sure to triple-lock it," she said.

He could hear the tremor in her voice. She'd been truly frightened. Once again, he was glad she could let herself show her fear. False bravado had gotten more than one person killed in his experience. He snapped the locks shut and checked that they were secure.

"All set," he said in his most reassuring tone, "and the apartment is all clear."

She was standing in the middle of the living room floor with her coat and gloves still on. Dampness filmed her forehead. Old, steam-heated buildings like this one could be too hot in the winter, especially on the lower floors. Even the hallway had been close to stifling.

"Let me take your coat," he said.

Delia jerked away from his reach. "Tell me what's going on here first. Was all of that outside for real, or are you just trying to convince me you're earning your pay?"

"It was real. Somebody attempted to get into this apartment sometime since we left this morning."

"What are you talking about? I didn't see any sign of that."

"It's the oldest trick in the book," he said. "I put a tiny strip of paper in the door just below the latch when we were leaving this morning. When we got back, I could see that the paper had slipped down the crack, as if somebody had been trying the knob and pulling at the door. And there are scrape marks around the keyholes that weren't there before. I'd say somebody tried to pick your locks. I'd also say it wasn't a pro."

"How do you know that?"

"A pro would have noticed the slip of paper trick and put it back where he found it. He also wouldn't have left scratches on the plate, and he'd probably have gotten through that first tumbler lock, maybe the second one, too."

"Great!" she said sarcastically. "That's really reassuring."

"He probably wouldn't have made it through the police lock." This wasn't entirely true and depended on what kind of equipment the B and E artist had with him, but she didn't need to know that just now. "Besides, like I said, it wasn't a pro."

"That's good to know."

She pulled off her gloves and began unbuttoning her coat.

"Why? Would you expect this Benno guy to hire somebody to come after you?"

She looked at Nick for a minute then looked away, as if she might be deciding what to tell him. He'd noticed her doing that a few other times when he'd asked her about Benno. Nick strongly suspected there was something she hadn't told him. He was running up against that wall of client secrets again. He hadn't expected such resistance from her. She was in the personal security business, after all. She must know that an important key to being effectively protected is full disclosure. What *he* knew was that direct questioning could push her even further under wraps. He'd bide his time for now and see what surfaced on its own.

"I don't know what Clyde is capable of." She slipped her coat off and tossed it over the chair arm. "It's hot in here," she said, maybe to divert the subject, and moved in the direction of the closed windows.

"Don't do that!"

Nick jumped in front of her and grabbed the hand she'd extended to lift the window latch. She'd been in motion when he intercepted her. Her final step put her very close to him, almost flat against his chest, with him still gripping her hand. Her face was tilted upward toward his. Her eyes inquired yet again what was going on here. Suddenly he found himself very aware of her mouth, only inches from his, close enough for him to see how the heat of the room had misted her upper lip. The urge to pull her into his arms came fierce and fast and straight from his groin. Her lips were full and slightly parted, as if she might have felt the same surge of desire. He pulled back from her and dropped her hand like it was a hot coal.

"Stay away from the windows," he said in a huskier tone than was usual for him, "especially these, since they overlook the front of the building. There's a clear line of vision into this apartment from the park. It would be best to keep the lights turned off in this part of the room, too."

"Can we open the windows?" she asked. "It's way too hot in here."

"Yes, it is." The temperature had vaulted even higher for him in the last few minutes. "I'll open them for you."

He was glad for the opportunity to stop facing her and move toward the windows. He checked carefully around the blinds. He didn't see anybody suspicious in the park or the street so he reached through the bars of the window gate to unlock the latch on the casing and ease the bottom half of the window up from the sill. He repeated the same cautious operation with the second window.

"I'll check the bedroom windows, too," he said.

"What about the blue spruce?"

"I'll bring it in as soon as I've checked the rest of the windows."

"I can probably manage the tree by myself," she said, and made a move toward the door.

He stepped in front of her but was careful not to touch her this time.

"Delia, please," he said. "Let me do my job."

She looked into his eyes for a moment. He was tempted to turn away. Her gaze threatened to get that fierce urge started in his groin again. Then she nodded and he was free to escape into the bedroom, at least for a short while. He heaved a sigh of relief as soon as he was out of her sight. He had to clamp a rein on himself right now. She was a beautiful woman, and it was natural for a man to be turned on by her. He, however, had a bottom line to attend to. That bottom line had nothing to do with nature and everything to do with business. Nick cranked his head back and forth to ease the tension in his neck and shoulders. He needed to plant his butt on that bottom line right now and keep it there for the duration.

As a first step in fulfilling that resolve, he walked to the bedroom window and pulled the cord to raise the blind just enough so he could see the outside sill. There he saw what he was looking for but had hoped he wouldn't find. This was the window onto the fire escape. The opening was gated on the inside like the rest but with a release mechanism to allow for quick exit in case of a fire. Nick wasn't interested in that mechanism at the moment. His attention was riveted on the sill.

"Delia," he called loudly enough to be heard in the living room. "Could you come in here, please?"

She didn't answer. Instead she was at his side almost instantly.

"What is it?" she asked, sounding anxious again, as she had when they'd first entered the apartment from the hallway.

"Do you see what I see on the windowsill?"

Nick pointed toward the glass to show her where to look. She examined the spot he'd indicated.

"It's a handprint, isn't it?" she asked.

The print was plainly visible in the sun's reflection off the greased surface.

"Yes, and it wasn't there when I checked last night."

"That means somebody was on my fire escape since then, maybe even last night while I was sleeping."

Nick nodded. "Most likely this morning. The same person who tried the door." He gestured toward the glass once more. "Is there anything else you notice about the print?"

"What do you mean?" she asked after examining the sill again.

"The size of it," he said. He'd moved around her toward the window so he'd have a clear visual angle on her face. "It's from a woman's hand. A small woman. What do you make of that?"

Delia didn't reply. She didn't avoid his gaze, either. She stared back at him with her face such a blank canvas that he had to wonder what she was erasing from his view.

Chapter Six

"This guy who's after you. Is he married?"

Nick had dragged the tall evergreen into the apartment from the hallway and used his pocketknife to cut the cords that bound the tree. At the moment he was holding it up straight while Delia twisted the screws of the green metal stand into the base of the trunk. She'd kept him busy in the hope that he'd forget the question he'd asked in the bedroom about the handprint on her windowsill. She'd had no answer then. The print definitely couldn't belong to the man who'd followed her from the office last night. So, whose could it be? What woman would climb three flights up a cold, slippery fire escape to try Delia's window? Nick had found more evidence—greasy fingerprints on the window itself. The gates probably discouraged whoever it was from breaking the glass. But, why a woman? That was Delia's question as well as Nick's. She needed a real answer for herself and a cover story answer for him. He'd just offered her the latter.

"Yes," she said. "I'm afraid he is."

One problem with lies is that it takes a lot of thought and planning to make sure you're telling the right one. Otherwise you may have to live with the consequences for a very long time. Delia knew this better than most people. Her entire life was a made-up story, and there'd been plenty of consequences to live with because of that.

"You sound relieved," Nick said.

"I suppose I am relieved."

"Why's that?"

Delia's position at the base of the tree saved her from having to look him in the face as she continued telling nontruths, half truths and barely truths.

"It's always a relief to bring a guilty secret out into the open," she said.

"I see."

Delia finished turning the screws—first one, then the next, then the last—till they were each equally anchored into the trunk to balance the tree and hold it upright. It occurred to her that she had to maintain the same kind of precarious balance with her life of deception. Otherwise everything could come toppling down. She got up from the floor and brushed off the slacks she'd worn to work today in case she needed to be more ready for action than a skirt allowed. Blue spruce needles clung to the dark wool, especially at the knees and below. She didn't mind. It was worth a stiff brushing to have the tree here, scenting her little hideaway with reminders of deep, quiet forests in a cleaner, simpler place.

"Then you do think it's wrong."

"What?"

Delia was still brushing her pants and musing about the tree. The significance of what he was saying eluded her for the moment.

"You said this was a guilty secret. That must mean you think you were doing something wrong."

She continued to stare at him with what she knew had to be a dumb look on her face. They were getting into a territory in which she had to be careful what she said and even more careful what she lied. She chose to say nothing at all for the moment.

"Getting involved with a married man..." Nick went on, though she wished he'd drop the subject. He was obviously intent upon prying a response out of her and probably wouldn't quit till he did. "You know that's not a right thing to do."

She actually agreed with that statement, but something in his tone suddenly shot her back up as straight as the trunk of the tree he was still holding.

"I believe that issues of right and wrong have to be decided by each person for him- or herself on a case-by-case basis depending on the circumstances." She knew that sounded like a line from either an ethics textbook or a TV talk show, but she didn't care.

"I see."

She hated the way he kept saying that.

"You see what?" she snapped.

He let go of the tree trunk and pulled his hand out from among the evergreen branches. She'd made him put on gloves while holding the tree so he wouldn't be scraped by the branches and needles. He pulled the gloves off slowly now and didn't speak till he'd walked over to his suede jacket, which he'd left on the couch before starting with the tree, and stuffed the gloves into one of the pockets. With every second of this slow, deliberate process on his part, Delia grew more irritated.

"What I see," he said finally, turning toward her again, "is that thinking the way you do about right and wrong amounts to changing the rules according to what's convenient for you at the moment."

"I didn't mean that at all."

"What did you mean then?"

He sounded perfectly calm while she was getting more and more agitated.

"I meant that what a person decides to do with her life is her personal business, and she shouldn't have to be preached to by some pompous jerk who thinks he knows all of the answers."

She saw the smile beginning on his face and wished she could reach out and rip it off. Where did he get the nerve to smirk at her?

"I'm not very much in favor of pompous jerks myself," he said in a suddenly softened tone that was tailor-made to disarm. "Especially when I'm being one myself."

The heat of Delia's anger was ready to explode all over the room, the blue spruce, and Nick Avery in particular. His words threatened to deflate that anger much more gradually and without damage. Delia wasn't sure she wanted that. A good blowup might be just what the doctor ordered. She could scream and yell, throw something at the wall. She could let out all the tension of these past two days, maybe even the past five years, in one colossal eruption, then worry about the resulting devastation later. That might be preferable to pounding her pillow and sobbing her heart out all by herself. One or the other needed to happen for her, and fairly soon.

"Let's start this conversation over again," he was saying while she decided whether to stick a cork in her temper or let it blow. "Hey, Ms. Barry, this is one really beautiful tree you've got here. Sheds a little." He displayed his needle-encrusted sweater sleeve for her to see. "But then, none of us is perfect."

He'd taken on a pointedly jocular tone, and the look in his eyes seemed to be asking her for forgiveness. Delia took a deep breath, held it a moment, then sighed a long exhale. It looked like she might have to find some other outlet for those pent-up emotions of hers, after all.

"You may have to wait for hanging the tinsel on 'er, though." He went on charming Delia out of her tantrum. "These branches are frozen harder than—"

"Harder than an angry woman's heart," she cut in.

At another moment they might have laughed together. Feelings had run too high for that this time. He only nodded and smiled as he picked needles from his sweater.

"I don't have time for decorating now, anyway," Delia said, checking her watch. "I have an appointment to keep."

"Then I'll be keeping it with you," Nick said, back in his bodyguard mode. "Where are we going?"

"The Lower East Side."

"What kind of business could you have down there?" He didn't sound pleased, probably because she was talking about a pretty rough neighborhood.

"It's not business this time. I tutor at a literacy center in the Hester Street Settlement House. I'm down there once a week, sometimes more."

"Could you call it off for a week or so, till we get this Clyde Benno thing cleared up?"

"I can't do that." Delia understood his concern, but she couldn't bring herself to do what he was asking. "These people I work with have had too many disappointments in their lives already. I can't let them down, especially not at Christmastime."

He studied her face for a moment. Then it was his turn to heave a sigh.

"Okay. The Lower East Side it is," he said, "but could we try to get there in the daylight?"

"Sure. We'll leave right now." Delia didn't remind him of how early it gets dark in late December. He'd figure that out for himself soon enough.

Nick pulled on his jacket. "I don't want to start another argument, but I do need to clarify something about that handprint on the windowsill."

Delia stopped at the bedroom doorway on her way to make a quick change into something more appropriate for Hester Street.

"What would you like to clarify?"

"Is it possible that the person you saw following you last night could have been a woman?"

Delia paused to check her memory one more time. "No," she said. "It was definitely a man."

"I see."

He said that with concern in his voice this time. Maybe that was why Delia didn't think to be irritated.

"That means we're dealing with two people then," he said.

"Yes," she said. "I know."

She went into the bedroom and shut the door behind her. She was careful not to let herself look in the direction of the windowsill.

NICK INSISTED they take a cab yet again, this time to the settlement house. Delia tried to tell him that would only make them more conspicuous, a violation of the invisibility rule for staying undercover if she'd ever heard one. Not many people took cabs on Hester Street. She certainly never had. The subway came close enough with a brisk walk added on, but Nick wouldn't hear of it. She understood his concern. He was only trying to do his job. Right now, that job was protecting her. She did appreciate how conscientious he was being about it, especially now that there might be two pursuers to look out for instead of one. She hadn't said anything to Nick yet, but she suspected that her next encounter with whoever was after her could be a violent one. She wasn't sure why she anticipated that, more intuition than anything concrete. She hadn't mentioned these thoughts to Nick simply because they were so unfounded. Besides, he might start asking more questions about her alleged ex-boyfriend. Intuition again, and common sense, told her the Clyde Benno story could wear thin with too much use so she avoided the subject as much as possible.

Unfortunately, the true story here was a lot scarier than the one Delia had made up. The person or persons she was actually afraid of had committed murder already, probably to get their hands on the money that would have been hers on her twenty-fifth birthday had she still been around to claim it. In just two more years, the other heirs could have her declared officially dead, as long as she didn't re-emerge as Rebecca Lester in the meantime. She didn't intend to do anything of the kind, but they wouldn't know that. Their interests would be best served by having her out of the way permanently, as in dead, rather than only underground somewhere. If she'd been spotted by someone or finally traced to her present location, as she'd always feared would happen someday, then she was in even greater danger than Nick believed. Delia would have preferred to take her chances with a psycho ex-lover, with or without an embittered spouse, than to find herself at the mercy of whoever had left poor Morty Lancer murdered in her bedroom five years ago.

Consequently, she hadn't given Nick too much of a hard time about the cab. Still, she couldn't resist a comment when he hopped out ahead of her in front of the settlement house and wouldn't let her follow until he'd thoroughly perused the street.

"Now everybody on the block thinks I'm either a felon being towed around by a cop or an heiress with so many valuables she needs somebody to check out the alleyways before she walks by."

"In that getup, you look more like the felon than the rich lady."

Nick was referring to her Hester Street outfit—ancient, faded jeans with rips at the knees backed by flannel patches and an I Luv NY sweatshirt that had started out white until it got mixed up in a load of dark laundry and turned an odd combo of several dingy colors. Brown leather hiking boots with heavy, tire-tread soles finished off her ensemble along with a banged-up leather bomber jacket that had become what they call "distressed" without any help from the manufacturer. Usually, she jammed a navy blue knit watch cap over her head and pulled it down over her ears. She hadn't done that today despite the biting weather. She told herself she didn't need a hat to ride in a cab. She understood, all the same, that her choice of bareheadedness had more to do with not looking like a stevedore in front of Nick than it did with anything else.

Maybe that's why she responded to him by asking, somewhat defensively, "What's wrong with my getup?"

He hustled her inside the door to the settlement house building before answering. "Not a thing, really." He looked her over, and she could feel her cheeks heat up from more than just being indoors. "You look very downtown," he said.

"Is that good or bad?"

His at least twice-over glance stopped at her eyes. "I imagine anything would look good on you."

They were standing just inside the door. There was plenty of activity here as always—a kid bouncing a basketball down the hallway, a social worker with an armload of manila folders talking with a police officer, a variety of other characters old and young. In an instant, all of that came to a halt for Delia, like in a dream or a movie where the background noise goes silent and the action becomes slow motion for a while. She hadn't expected Nick to answer her so directly or in such a serious tone. They'd been bantering up till then, on the way over here in the cab and coming into the building. Now he was standing there looking down at her with something in his eyes that froze her in fear and, at the same time, made her heart leap under her discolored sweatshirt. She was both relieved and disappointed when he broke the spell.

"You said you had an appointment here. Who's it with?" he asked.

"Her name is Jaycee." Delia was surprised to hear her voice work so well over the lump of tangled emotions in her throat. "She's probably waiting for me now. She never misses a lesson."

Delia took off down the hall in a hurry, both because she didn't want to be late for her session with Jaycee and to put some distance between herself and Nick. Right now, she needed that buffer zone against the way her body apparently couldn't stop responding to him at close quarters. Unfortunately he caught up and kept pace with her easily. There was no way to get away from him, short of breaking into a run. She wasn't about to resort to that, and he'd probably just start running himself if she did. She slowed her step to a speed more in sync with this generally pretty-laid-back place. They reached the room where she did her tutoring, and she was about to ask him to wait for her out here in the hallway when the door opened on Jaycee and her lopsided grin.

Delia wasn't sure if Jaycee smiled that way because she might have a stroke in her past medical history or from some kind of street injury to her face. She'd been no stranger to the violence that plagues those who live by their wits without permanent shelter in the city. Still, Delia had never once met with Jaycee that she didn't have that crooked smile on her face and a happy word to say.

"Hi, there, sugar. I was wonderin' if you'd be making it down here tonight, what with Christmas comin' and all."

"I wouldn't want to miss a lesson with you, Jaycee, and if I had to, I'd make sure I got a message to you in advance."

"And I 'preciate that, too, honey. I can't tell you how much. Now tell me, who's this handsome lad?"

Delia turned to see Nick eyeing Jaycee warily. Delia might have reacted similarly the first time she met Jaycee, except that by then Delia had been volunteering at Hester Street for quite some time and it no longer even occurred to her to expect the people here to look like they were turned out for a fashionable afternoon on Fifth Avenue. Still, she could understand what Nick might be thinking now.

Jaycee's appearance was eccentric to say the least. Her hair was wild, gray frizz that could never be quite contained by any of the various forms of headgear she chose to wear. Today's chapeau was a rather shabby Shriner's fez, complete with top tassel and Jaycee's own personal modification, flaps of red fabric sewn onto the rim and long enough to cover her ears. The rest of her costume generally consisted of all or most of the garments in her possession, worn in differing order from one of her meetings with Delia to the next. Today a once-blue denim drop-waisted dress was on top. From beneath the long hem protruded the boots Delia herself had scouted out at the big Salvation Army store on West Forty-sixth Street. She'd known better than to buy new boots, however much she wanted to. New boots would attract too much envious attention among Jaycee's fellow street dwellers.

The most extraordinary thing about Jaycee's appearance was how clean she was able to keep herself and her clothing, all the many layers of it. This was no mean feat for a woman with no bathroom to call her own. Delia respected Jaycee's privacy and didn't ask how she accomplished that feat. Public rest rooms, facilities here at the settlement house, quarters not easily come by hoarded for the coin-operated laundry. Delia suspected that Jaycee took advantage of all of these and any other opportunities to get to clean water and a little soap, as long as it didn't involve going to a city shelter. Jaycee had told Delia how dangerous those places were and vowed to stay out of them at all costs. Delia couldn't take Nick aside to tell him these things now. Instead she decided to have him sit in on the reading lesson, after all.

For the next two hours he stayed at the back of the room and watched while Jaycee struggled over one word after another but wouldn't let Delia help her much. Jaycee's determination to learn to read by her own diligence was as strong as her determination to maintain her personal hygiene and the dignity that went with it. By the end of the session, out of the corner of her eye, Delia could see Nick leaning forward in his chair mouthing the words he had already figured out just from listening, wanting to help Jaycee in her valiant struggle. Maybe Nick had learned a lesson of his own that day on Hester Street, Delia thought as the three of them walked down the hall to the front door of the settlement house at the end of the lesson.

"Oh, I almos' forgot," Jaycee said as Delia and Nick were about to leave. "I got a prediction for you. An important one."

"Jaycee is believed by many to have the power of future sight," Delia said to Nick in response to his questioning look. He nodded his head but didn't say anything. She could pretty much imagine his skeptical thoughts, since she had some of those herself—though she never mentioned them to Jaycee.

"What I see for you is two gifts," Jaycee said, "both comin' on Christmas Eve. One'll come from me. The other's gonna be from heaven." Jaycee folded her arms across her many-layered bosom and smiled crookedly. "You jus' keep your heart true, honey, and my sight's gonna prove true, too."

"Thanks, Jaycee. I'll keep that in mind."

"You got a true heart in you, whatever your secrets may be, sugar. I know that for a sure fact."

Delia was stopped short by that statement. If Nick hadn't been there, she would have asked Jaycee what secrets she was talking about, but Delia didn't want him to hear the answer. She didn't really believe in second sight, psychic powers, that sort of thing. But she didn't entirely disbelieve, either. She'd steer the subject in another direction if Nick brought up the predictions. Unfortunately, what he actually wanted to talk about after they'd left the settlement house was even touchier.

"Have you considered the possibility that your friend Jaycee could be the one trying to break into your place?" he asked.

"No, I haven't considered that." Delia sounded even more belligerent because she didn't want to believe that what he was suggesting could be true.

"I guess you weren't watching when she was pointing out the words she was reading with her finger."

"What are you talking about? Of course, I was watching."

"Then you should have noticed that Jaycee has very small hands."

Delia shrugged and turned toward the corner. She had suggested they walk to one of the wider thoroughfares where they'd be more likely to find a cab to flag down. They stepped off the curb in that direction. Nick might have made his customary visual sweep of the vicinity; Delia didn't notice. She was too disturbed by his observation about the size of Jaycee's hands and by the fact that it happened to be accurate. Delia also didn't notice the late-model, dark-colored car suddenly hurtling toward them until the last moment of possible safety. Then it was Nick's fast reaction and strong arms that saved her from being mowed down. He picked her up off her feet and spun backward to the curb in a single motion that carried them both out of the path of death just in the nick of time.

After the dark sedan had sped off down the street, Delia clung to Nick's jacket and gasped for each terrified breath with his arms around her, and very welcome. He didn't have to say that this wasn't likely to have been an accident. She didn't have to say that Jaycee, the homeless woman from the settlement house, wasn't likely to have been the person behind the wheel.

Chapter Seven

Nick couldn't believe he didn't get the license plate number. They were under a streetlight when it happened, and he missed the tag. He didn't give chase, either. Those things were usually second nature to him, but not today. When that car came bearing down on them out of nowhere, there'd been nothing in his nature—or his mind and heart—but Delia. He could say he was doing his job, protecting the client, but he knew that wasn't why he'd forgotten every lawman instinct he'd ever had to pick her up in his arms and shield her with his body till the danger had passed. She'd huddled trembling against him while he'd murmured comfort into the sweet scent of her hair.

Because of that, they had nothing to go on now when it came to proving Benno, or his wife, tried to run Delia down. The streetlight made mistaken identity extremely unlikely. The way the car veered to the right from its direct path confirmed that this was a deliberate attempt to hit her. Otherwise, Nick had no evidence and, of course, there'd been no witnesses. They were in a part of town where nobody sees anything, especially when it involves strangers. That meant no details on the driver except a description of a dark sedan that could have been any of a thousand cars.

As if all of that wasn't bad enough, he'd let Delia have her way when she'd insisted they come straight home. Again, he hadn't been using his cop's good judgment. At the time, he could only think about taking her where she'd feel safe. Still, he knew very well that this apartment, even with all of her security measures, was the last place she should seek refuge. Both Benno and his wife would expect her to come here. Nick had tried to tell Delia that, but she wasn't being rational right now. He could understand how shaken and terrified she had to be. He'd been pretty scared for her himself, too scared to be as cool and calculating as he usually was on a case. All he could focus on was keeping her in the shelter of his arms from that corner of Hester Street back here to her apartment. Even now that they were inside, with the locks engaged and the heavy drapes pulled shut, he didn't want to let her go. He wished he could hold on to her forever. The startling nature of that thought was what finally allowed him to step away from her side.

"We need to get the police involved now," he said after he had her settled on the couch with a cup of hot tea in her hand and a blanket tucked around her.

"No police," she said.

She'd been saying that from the first time he'd suggested it in the Sea Grill. She was even more adamant now.

"He tried to run you over with his car," Nick insisted just as emphatically while he paced her small living room. "By the way, was that his car?"

"What?"

She looked up at him with a vague expression on her face, like she was still too knocked off kilter by what had happened to comprehend his words. Nick forced his cop sense to overrule the urge to run to her side and fold her into his arms again. He'd done enough of that already. It was time for other, more deliberately defensive action now.

"I asked if you recognized Benno's car."

"I guess so." She sounded vague, too. "I couldn't really be sure. It was dark."

He wouldn't argue with her while she was in such a frazzled state, but they'd been beneath the streetlight. Still, he let it pass for the moment.

"If we went to the police, they could check out the exact model of his car so we'd know if it fits the general description of the one we'd seen tonight. You do know what he drives, don't you?"

"We're not going to the police. How many times do I have to say that?"

Her hands were shaking again, hard enough to make the teacup rattle in its saucer.

"Okay, okay," Nick said. He'd have to change his approach here. "Then let me go after Benno at his home. You said he lives out on Long Island. Right?"

"You're not going to do that. You're going to stick with me and be my bodyguard. That's what I hired you to do. It isn't your job to play detective, or strong-arm man, either."

She sounded like she was back in control, as if the effort to make herself heard by him was bringing her to her normal self again. But that wasn't what captured Nick's attention most. What came through to him loud and clear was the rightness of what she'd said about the nature of his job. A bodyguard stuck with the client first and foremost. He didn't go running off to hunt down the perp. Nick might have been a cop a long time ago, but he wasn't one anymore and hadn't been for almost ten years. There was no excuse for forgetting that. The client and the client's wishes had priority, and that included going along with her if she wanted to keep the law out of her business. Many people who hire personal protection do so for just that reason, to avoid official intrusion and inquiries into their private concerns. Delia had every right to want that, too.

"You win," he said, and halted his pacing to sit down next to her on the couch. He took the cup and saucer from her and put them on the end table. She'd taken only a sip or two, and the tea had gone cold. "We won't go to the police, and I won't go after Benno. But I am going to insist on some other aggressive precautions."

"What would those precautions be?"

She sounded strong again, more like herself. Still, Nick would have loved to put his arms around her once more.

"First of all, I want you to move out of this place for a while."

"Where would I go?"

"Don't you have some family somewhere?"

"No family," she said, pulling the blanket closer around her.

"What about all of those people over there?"

Nick gestured toward the photographs on the claw-footed table by the window. Once again, she didn't seem to comprehend what he was saying to her. She was apparently still more shaken than he'd thought, which would be natural for somebody who narrowly escaped death only an hour ago.

"They're all too far away," she said after a moment, averting her eyes from the photos, as if she couldn't stand to be reminded of the long distance she was from home. "Besides, I have no intention of leaving the city."

He could hear that she was refusing to let this guy run her out of town. Nick had to admire and respect the courage of that conviction.

"Then we'll move you somewhere else in Manhattan for a few days. Benno may cool down some in the meantime."

"What kind of move are you thinking of?"

"Someplace where there's good security, like a hotel."

Nick had lived in hotels himself for so long that it was almost automatic for him to think of them as a residence alternative. Delia didn't say anything. She looked like she might be allowing the idea to settle in. At least, she didn't start right off with a negative response as she had with his other suggestions. He shut his mouth and let her think quietly. She could be very stubborn. He'd already found that out about her. Now that the shock of Hester Street was wearing off and she was returning to normal, that characteristic stubbornness could pop up like a wall between them at any moment. If he pushed her too hard, he could make that happen, which was the last thing he wanted.

Nick settled back against the couch cushions and watched her clasp and unclasp her hands in her lap. She had beautiful hands, pale-skinned and tapered and rather delicate. That thought caught in Nick's investigative mind like a piece of silk on a snag. Were her hands about the same size as the prints on the windowsill? Was there any possibility she could have made those marks herself? If so, why would she do that?

Nick shook himself mentally. Exactly. Why would she do that? She had no reason. His automatically suspicious mind, long trained to find deception everywhere, was working overtime again. This was a case of unrequited love gone haywire, with a jealous mate thrown in for good measure. The stalking lover angle was something of a different wrinkle on the theme but not by much. Stalkers were getting to be as commonplace as outraged spouses these days. Nick had no reason to read anything more than that into this case. Besides, now that he thought about it, Delia's fingers were longer than the ones in the prints on the windowsill and window. He let himself dwell for a moment on how much he'd like to cover those hands with his own and what her reaction might be if he did. He was still thinking about that when she finally spoke.

"A hotel might be a good idea," she said. "One of the first-class ones where they keep a large security staff and a tight safety net because they have so many high-powered guests."

She seemed to be musing to herself as much as she was talking to him. Nick spoke quietly so as not to interrupt her thoughtful and, at last, calmer mood.

"Did you have someplace specific in mind?" he asked.

"The Waldorf," she said with the finality of someone who has come upon the perfect solution to a problem.

Nick was stunned into silence for a moment. He'd expected something a little less grand.

"Wouldn't that be a bit pricey?" he asked. She was only an office manager, after all. How much money could she make?

"Pricey?" She seemed to come suddenly back from wherever her mind had been off to. "Oh, I belong to the Hilton Club. They give you free nights and special rates. The Waldorf's a Hilton Hotel now."

She would know about hotels, of course. She had to put clients up in them sometimes. As for the Hilton Club, Nick knew about frequent traveler plans. He wondered where she'd traveled to get enough points for free nights in a place like the Waldorf. Most of all, he couldn't help wondering who'd taken those trips with her. Could it have been this Benno character? He takes off on what he tells his wife is a business junket and sneaks his other woman along. Nick grimaced to himself at the thought. So far, he'd been doing a pretty good job of keeping himself from connecting Delia sexually with Benno. He didn't want to start making those connections now.

"The Waldorf it is," Nick said.

DELIA KNEW she'd almost blown her cover with that question about the Waldorf. So much was going on that she'd forgotten for a moment to watch out for the details of her daily life cover story. She was generally careful to keep her spending habits realistic for her alleged salary level, which wasn't difficult for her. She was content with a small, simple apartment. She no longer wore jewels like the ones she'd taken with her when she'd fled Colorado. She'd used those expensive trinkets to set herself up in business and begin a modest investment portfolio. Not bad for Becky Lester, a flighty twenty-something who wasn't supposed to have a brain in her head. As Delia Barry, she'd taught herself to manage those investments wisely to build a solid financial foundation. Most of all, Delia had worked. The result was that she could well afford the Waldorf-Astoria Hotel.

On the other hand, for Delia Marie, office functionary, such accommodations would be more than a pinch. Considering that, she'd resisted the impulse to take a two-bedroom suite and booked them into two regular, but adjoining rooms.

"We're all set," she said as she dashed around her apartment, throwing things into one duffel and a single suit bag.

"Good. I want to get out of here tonight."

"What about your things? Or do you travel with what you can carry on your back?" Like some ancient vagabond or Old West cowboy, she couldn't help thinking.

"I'll stop back at my place later to pick up my kit."

Delia decided he might be the modern day version of a high plains drifter after all, which gave her even more reason to want him installed in that adjoining room. She needed a hired gun on her side right now. More than she would have admitted out loud to him or anyone else, she was afraid.

She remembered this kind of fear as a version of what she'd experienced that morning five years ago. Her breath came high in the back of her throat, and she could barely swallow over the dryness there. At some moments the fear would rev itself up to panic pitch, as if she were in the middle of a nightmare not knowing which way to run since every direction led to disaster. All of her will and determination had to be pressed into service to wrestle that frenzy back under control. Otherwise chaos could break through onto the surface. Then she was actually likely to go darting off, this way and that, and back again. Even with all of her control instincts engaged, she could feel her breath high and shallow, as if she'd been doing that furtive dashing about in more than just her imagination.

Nonetheless, she hated leaving her apartment, being chased out of the home she'd made for herself. She'd felt safe there till now, tucked up in her cozy nest of three warm rooms. Unfortunately she wasn't safe there any longer. She understood that even more clearly than Nick did. Whoever was after her had strong reasons for wanting her dead. A pile of money was at stake, multiples of her tidy investment portfolio and PEI's profit margin combined. Working for rich clients these past five years made her very aware of how far some people will go to get their hands on that kind of money and what lengths they will take to keep from losing it. She had no doubt at all that her pursuers, as soon as they wangled a clear opportunity to do so, would kill her, and maybe Nick, too. Delia was not too proud to admit that thought terrified her.

So she'd packed her bags to go into hiding. Her heart saddened as she took one last look at the blue spruce still standing bare-branched in her living room. She'd so looked forward to arranging colored lights and draping garland. She'd also looked forward to doing that with some company this year. She could see Nick, in her mind's eye at least, disentangling the light strings while she unpacked glass Christmas balls from their tissue storage wrappings. She imagined his chiseled silhouette in the halo of twinkling tree lights and could almost hear the carols she played each Christmas Eve. She'd played those carols all by herself for several seasons now. In the last twenty-four hours she'd come to remember what it was like not to be by herself any longer. She'd been lonely these past five years, sometimes desperately so. No amount of hard work and keeping busy could cover up that reality. Before yesterday, she might have been able to tell herself she was settled into her hermit's life and resigned to staying there. Tonight, she understood how untrue that was. Thus, trimming the tree had taken on even more importance for her than usual.

FORTUNATELY, the Waldorf had gone out of its way to make the season bright. The grand chandelier in the foyer sparkled with light. This already majestic cascade of twinkling glass prisms had been left free of holiday festoonery, but the rest of the foyer made up for that one concession to simplicity. Sculpted shrubs in pots were wound around with burgundy velvet and gold net sashing. A tableau in motion depicted an eighteenth-century street scene, circa the era of the original Waldorf-Astoria. Huge poinsettia plants in brass tureens lined the railing above the marble entrance stairs. Delia stopped for a moment and turned almost full circle in the middle of the famous Wheel of Life mosaic. There it was—up on the balcony near the lobby piano lounge—a lovely tree so tall it barely cleared the ceiling. The tree had been draped in more velvet sash, hung with large gilded pinecones, then twined the full length in woven vines of winter brown.

"Isn't it all so very beautiful," she breathed, hardly aware that at the moment she sounded about eight years old.

"Yes, it is," Nick answered.

The stillness of his tone prompted her to complete her circling in his direction. He wasn't extolling the splendor of the foyer. He was looking directly at her, and she suspected he'd been doing so all along. Delia dropped her glance and felt her cheeks warm in a blush that would have suited the bonneted young lady in the nearby Victorian tableau. Delia had noticed Nick admiring her before but never so openly as now. Her long winter overcoat was suddenly too warm beneath his gaze. She fumbled to undo the buttons as she walked toward the main lobby with more haste than might have been usual for a place as genteel as the Waldorf.

The events of the past twenty-four hours had consumed her mind so completely that she'd had little time for pondering the present much less the past. Even in their few tranquil moments she'd kept herself from thinking much about the fact that she'd once been infatuated enough with Nick to want him for her lover. Now she had to stifle an impulse toward panic, as she realized how difficult it might be to continue suppressing that past desire with the two of them staying in the same hotel together, only a door's width apart.

Chapter Eight

All the time the bellman was fussing about to get Delia settled, she couldn't take her eyes off the door to the adjoining room. She let the bellman open her bag and hang up her clothes. She always did that kind of thing for herself, but the longer he stayed here, the longer it would be before she had to deal with that door and the man on the other side of it. In the confined space of the elevator on the way up to this floor, she'd found Nick more attractive than ever against the rich glow of mahogany and polished brass. She'd reacted exactly this same way to him five years ago. She'd hoped she would have outgrown that by now, especially since she prided herself on being an in-control person these days. Yet, there she was in that elevator, in such an intense state of agitation she had to step backward out of his visual range in case her discomfort might show. She'd greeted the arrival of their floor with profound relief. Now, being in the same room with that adjoining door promised to make the elevator ride seem like child's play.

A tune danced through her head. ''I've been lonely too long.'' Not exactly a holiday carol, but apropos to the moment to be sure.

Meanwhile, the bellman had finished hanging her clothes from the suit bag and was unzipping her duffel.

"That's okay," she said. "I'll take care of those."

She couldn't have a stranger unpacking her underwear, no matter how much she needed the company. She went to the bed where she'd left her shoulder bag and fumbled for her wallet and a tip big enough to guarantee good service during her stay here but not so big as to appear ostentatious. Where had she learned to make that distinction? Her hand froze on the smooth leather of her wallet. Her father taught her that.

"Are you all right, miss?"

The bellman's concerned tone brought Delia back to the present scene. She could all but see herself, freeze-framed still as a statue, staring into space with her hand stuck in her bag.

"Fine," she said, though that definitely was not true. She pulled a bill from her wallet and handed it to the bellman. "Thanks for your help." She tried her best to arrange her face into what would be considered an appropriate expression. Unfortunately at the moment she couldn't quite recall what that appropriate expression might be.

The bellman glanced surreptitiously down at his palm and said, "Thank *you*."

His tone made Delia wonder about the size of the bill she'd given him. At least Nick Avery had managed to make one person happy today. As for herself, Nick appeared to be turning her into an airhead more decidedly by the minute. In direct contradiction to what she'd been thinking only moments ago, she was now relieved when the bellman walked out the door and left her by herself. It occurred to her that she'd handled Nick's presence better when they were about to be run down by

a car. When they were in peril, she was out on the edge
of her nerve endings without time or inclination to think
about what the rest of her psyche, not to mention her
hormones, was doing. The mistake was to allow herself
to feel relatively safe as she did now. That put her in a
different kind of danger.

First of all, she was being assaulted by the past, by
pieces of the personal history she'd taught herself to
keep under wraps so she wouldn't have to feel the pain.
Her father was one of those painful memories she kept
carefully compartmentalized. That way, she didn't have
to think about how much she'd loved him and what a
joy it would be to have him with her now as she felt her
own strength wobble beneath her like legs after a sea
voyage. He'd been the rock the sea smashed against but
never budged. He would know what to do in this situation. That thought stopped Delia in her tracks yet
again. What would he have told her to do here? What
did she remember him telling her to do, time and time
again from when she was barely tall enough to see over
his knee till the day his helicopter made its final takeoff?

"Lead with the truth, and you'll walk a straight
path," he would say.

The past five years had hardly been a straight path for
her, dodging off at a tangent into the shadows when-
ever anyone came too close, giving crooked answers to
what for other people were simple, forthright questions. Now she was hip-deep in a lie to Nick. She needed
his help desperately. Yet she couldn't be truthful with
him about why she needed his help. Even more frus-
trating, was the impossibility of letting him know how
she really felt about him. Most women had to worry
about wearing their hearts on their sleeves for fear the

men in their lives might run for the hills. Delia's fear was that, if Nick knew the truth about who she was, he might run to the police. Nonetheless, all of a sudden she was struck by the impulse to charge over to that adjoining door, knock on it until he appeared, then tell him the whole truth and nothing but the truth. To her credit, she still had just enough brain cells functioning to know what a bad move that kind of full disclosure would be. She headed for the exit into the hallway instead and almost made it there.

If Delia had been less upset by the presence of the door into Nick's room, she probably wouldn't have jumped and screamed when it opened just as she was passing. Unfortunately, for the status of her dignity at least, jump and scream was precisely what she did. Even more unfortunately, she jumped straight into Nick's arms. Then, as if she must be totally intent upon making herself look like an utter fool, she began struggling like mad to escape his grasp. He'd clasped her by the shoulders, maybe to keep her from knocking him down when she leapt upon him. She twisted her body furiously back and forth, as if trying to extricate herself from a tight place. The harder she twisted, the harder he gripped.

"Delia, it's me," he said.

If he meant that to be reassuring he was having the opposite effect.

"Let go of me," she said, and struggled on.

"Delia, it's Nick."

The awareness was dawning that he thought she'd mistaken him for the alleged psycho boyfriend or his outraged wife and believed she was being accosted. She might have corrected that misapprehension, but he didn't give her the chance. He clamped his arms around her, pulled her close to his chest and began stroking her hair.

"Calm down," he said. "You're safe here with me."

He obviously intended to soothe her with those words and his ministrations to her hair. Even she understood how bewildered he had to be when she reacted as she did.

"Get your hands off me. I know who you are, and I want your hands off me."

Between that vehement cry and his releasing her, a few seconds lapsed during which he was most likely attempting to figure out what particular bee she might have in her bonnet now. Then he let her go and stepped back, almost into the door that was still ajar to the next room. He lifted his palms at arm's length between them, either as a placating gesture or to protect himself against what must have seemed to him the unaccountable fury that had her trembling visibly in front of him.

"See?" he said, spreading his extended arms wider. "My hands are off. Will you calm down now and tell me what has you so rattled? Did something happen?"

The confusion in his eyes was probably what brought Delia back to terra firma. He hadn't a clue what was going on here. Not a breath of an intimation of a hint of what she was feeling about him had entered his mind, which made her want to laugh. If she hadn't bitten her lip at that very moment, so hard she could almost taste her own blood, she would in fact have broken into peals of hilarity on the spot. Thank heaven she had her wits sufficiently about her to understand that there would have been more hysteria in that laughter than she wanted Nick, or even herself, to hear. Also, at the same instant, she was being moved toward tears. If he hadn't guessed how attracted she was to him a good deal of the reason could be because he felt no such attraction to her, which made her want to cry.

"I'm not rattled," she said in a defiant tone, all the time knowing this to be one of the most absurd statements she'd ever made.

"I see."

There he was "seeing" everything again, when she knew for an absolutely incontrovertible truth that he saw nothing. Her fury threatened to reignite. If she permitted that to happen, she'd be in danger of coming off as a complete crazy woman.

"I need to get out of this room," she said. She was forcing herself to appear calm, which, for some unfathomable reason, made her voice come out in what most closely resembled a squeak.

"Where did you have in mind to go?"

He was still watching her carefully, but his expression had gravitated from bewilderment to wariness.

"Go?" she squeaked as if that might be the most ridiculous question she'd ever heard. She cleared her throat before speaking again and managed to bring her pitch down half an octave or so. "I had no specific destination in mind. I thought maybe I'd just wander around the hotel for a while."

"To get your bearings and scout the premises?"

"Exactly."

She was grateful that he'd come up with such a rational explanation. Despite her father's sage advice, she'd have been hard-pressed to tell the truth right now. How could she admit that, in point of fact, the mere sight of a door had sent her plummeting headlong in the opposite direction from rationality. Such a confession was definitely not the way to go in her quest to knit together the remaining threads of her dignity.

"Fine," he said, "but I have to go with you."

"You do?" She wished she couldn't hear how silly that sounded.

"I'm your bodyguard. Remember? A bodyguard covers the body."

Delia managed only a nod in response to that as she headed the rest of the way to the hallway door, wishing he hadn't chosen quite those words.

NICK HAD NO idea what could be wrong with Delia. He only knew he shouldn't leave her alone. When she took off down the hall out of her room, he followed. She was walking so fast he had to hustle to keep up. Luckily for them, the corridor was empty or she would definitely have attracted more attention than was wise to do. They were here to hide, after all, not to be noticed. Their outfits might have gotten them more attention than he preferred even without Delia darting off down the hall as if she had the devil on her tail.

They certainly didn't look like they belonged at the Waldorf. He would have changed clothes if he'd had the chance to stop back at his hotel. There'd been no time for that so he still had on his jeans and dark sweater. He'd left his jacket in his room. At least, Delia'd taken off those hobnailed boots she'd worn to Hester Street. The pair she was wearing now were made of soft, black leather that hugged her narrow foot and had a short, square heel. She'd gotten rid of the sweatshirt and patched jeans, too, which was probably a good idea, though he missed how endearing she'd looked in them. Before leaving her apartment, she'd put on a sweater, also soft and also black and very well made. He guessed it was cashmere. The red in her hair shone against the dark wool as she hurried toward the elevators.

He wanted to tell her to slow down and think through what she was doing and where she was going, but he could see she was still very agitated. She clutched her arms around herself and stared impatiently at the floor indicator as they waited for the elevator. She shifted from one foot to the other and bit her lip. She was obviously not in a frame of mind to be reasoned with right now. He didn't have to be an expert on human nature to figure that out. Nick kept his mouth shut and followed her into the elevator when it finally arrived.

They weren't alone. A thirty-something couple stood at the back of the car. Nick smiled to reassure them that they weren't suddenly in the company of Bonnie and Clyde. The couple had their coats on as if they planned to go outside. They looked like they were from out of town. The woman had on too much jewelry for the casual outfit she was wearing, and especially for the streets of Manhattan. Most men might not notice such things. Careful observation was part of Nick's training and his job, as was making judgments and deductions about the people he and his clients encountered.

He was tempted to tell this woman to go back to her room, take off some of that jewelry and make the rest less conspicuous if she was going out onto the street. He resisted the impulse. He was here to take care of Delia and nobody else, which was proving to be a very full-time assignment. Besides, this woman probably wouldn't appreciate his advice anyway. She most likely wouldn't listen, either. She'd just finished looking Delia's simple, understated outfit up and down with obvious distaste. The woman shifted her gaze to Nick. He saw a flash of approval in her eyes as she checked him out from his boots on up. Still, he suspected she wouldn't consider either himself or Delia a reliable fashion consultant.

They rode down to the lobby level in silence. Nick took note that Delia had managed to calm the more blatant signals of her agitated state, probably for the benefit of the couple in the elevator. She stepped briskly out of the car after the doors slid open. Nick waited to see which way she'd go—to the left and the foyer at the front of the hotel or to the right and the main reception area. There were cocktail lounges in both directions and restaurants, too. Nick was definitely hungry. He hoped one of those restaurants was on Delia's itinerary. He was about to take a chance on reigniting her frenzy by suggesting they get something to eat, when she began behaving in what he considered a bizarre manner once more.

She'd stepped to the side of the elevator door and put her thumb on the call button, apparently to keep the car from moving, as if she were a hotel employee in charge of making sure the door stayed open while guests exited. She stood like that, almost patiently, as the tourist couple walked out. The woman glanced back as they continued toward the front foyer. She leaned toward the man she was with to say something, and he glanced back, too. They turned away again, both shaking their heads. Nick could all but hear them pegging Delia and himself as New York weirdos who were way out of their element at the Waldorf.

Meanwhile, Delia was doing something that made even Nick think that the tourist couple might be right in their judgment, at least of her. Instead of walking in one direction or another along the lobby, she'd stepped back into the elevator. The door began to close, probably because she now had her finger on the button to make it do that. Nick slipped through the narrowing opening just in time to keep from being either crushed between the doors or left in the lobby. She pushed a floor button. He looked at the panel. Number four was lighted. He wondered if she had a specific destination in mind. He didn't ask. He'd decided that the best approach was to let her calm down all the way. Movement, wherever it might lead them, could have that calming effect. Being interrogated would not.

She'd already cooled down some. The pinkish heat of excitement that had colored her throat and reddened her cheeks was subsiding. Nick found himself unable to turn his gaze away from the place where her black sweater met the white skin of her neck. He thought at first that the beauty of the contrast had him mesmerized, but there was something more. He couldn't quite put his finger on what this particular sight stirred in him. He pressed his memory for the connection, but the elevator stopped at the fourth floor before he had an answer.

Delia was out the door almost instantly at a furious pace, maybe in pursuit of whatever peace of mind she hoped these opulent corridors might have to offer. Nick understood that impulse. She wanted her life back. When some crazy was after you, that's what it felt like—as if your life had been, not just invaded, but stolen from you. Nick had heard other clients talk about having such feelings, and the rage and frustration that went with them. He suspected Delia might be feeling the same thing right now. If that sent her charging through hotel hallways like she'd been shot from a cannon, he was willing to trail along. Still, he was relieved when she slowed a few yards beyond the elevator door and allowed him to catch up.

"You may be wondering why I've gathered us together here this evening," she said when he joined her.

Her voice was surprisingly unemotional considering
her behavior since they'd left her room. She wasn't
smiling so Nick didn't recognize right away that she was
making a joke. He stared at her for a moment, wondering what she could be talking about. Then he got the
picture.

"Yes," he said. "I was wondering that very thing."

"I'll bet you were."

She still wasn't smiling, but she had definitely calmed
down, even rediscovered her sense of humor. Nick allowed himself to relax just a little. Then she did something even more unexpected than her previous dashing
around. She linked her arm through his and began
walking down the hall at a normal pace.

"We're a nice couple from somewhere sane, like
Tennessee or Texas or Idaho," she was saying. "We've
come to New York City for the holidays, and right now
we're exploring this fancy hotel we've checked into."

Nick understood that she was defining their cover—
what they should try to look like to other people. He
could also hear the nostalgia in her tone, as if she might
be wishing their circumstances really were so innocent
and uncomplicated. They passed a wide mirror on the
corridor wall and he stole a glance into it. They certainly did look like they could be that nice couple she
described. He was only a little surprised to hear his own
thoughts whisper a wish as nostalgic as she sounded.
Nick allowed himself only an instant of that. He had to
keep alert to the present, and that also didn't mean
thinking about how he could feel the soft warmth of her
breast brush against his upper arm as they walked
along.

He turned himself determinedly away from that sensation, and that was when he sensed something very different. He suddenly had the feeling they were being followed. He turned around and looked behind them. He didn't let go of her arm. Luckily, she was on his left side, which kept his weapon hand free. The gun in his back waistband was within easy reach. He was ready to go for it if he had to, but his backward glance revealed no need for such drastic action. The corridor was empty, just as it had been when they passed through it. Doorways led off to one side. He'd already figured out that this must be the conference room level of the hotel. Those double doorways had all been closed when he and Delia walked by, and there was no sound coming from beyond any of them. The only noise he could hear was in the other direction, the way they were headed but far off and not threatening.

"Is something wrong?" Delia asked.

His survey of the corridor behind them had disturbed their strolling pace. He felt her body begin to tense again beneath his arm. He didn't want that. Maybe the bodyguard manual would say it was good for a client to be scared onto her toes when she was a mark, but Delia'd been on her toes for so long now she was about ready to topple over.

"Just checking out the neighborhood. All's clear," he said, and hoped that was true.

Chapter Nine

Delia had been walking hallways and turning corners blindly ever since they left the elevator. She hoped Nick had some idea where they were now because she didn't. She'd have asked him about that, but she was afraid her voice would break. She didn't intend to let Nick know how shaken just being in the same corridor with him made her feel. Squeaking like a boy at puberty was sure to reveal exactly that, so she kept her mouth shut and silently hoped his compass was working better than hers at the moment.

Delia's agitation really began back at her apartment when he asked about the people in the photos on her window table. He naturally assumed they were her family. She'd wished she could blurt out the whole pathetic story of how she'd found those pictures in a box of old, framed photographs at a secondhand store and bought them for a dollar or two apiece. She hadn't known why she was doing that at the time, at least not consciously. When she got them home, she'd washed the glass and polished the brass frames till they gleamed. She'd set them up on that table with the window light behind them. She knew they weren't her actual family, of course, but it was easier to look at their faces than to remember the real ones and how much pain went along with those memories. She recognized now, more than she'd let herself before, how pitiful such a story would sound, especially to a man like Nick. Maybe that's why, when she heard music coming from down the hotel corridor ahead of them she took off, all but running toward the distraction.

A short flight of stairs brought them closer to the sound. She caught a glimpse of herself in the mirror above the stairs then looked quickly away. Her cheeks were too flushed, and her eyes were too bright. She had the appearance of being just a little crazed, but that wasn't what made her turn her glance away. Nick was only a couple of steps behind her. She saw concern in his eyes, and that made her feel more unhinged than ever.

At the bottom of the stairs and to the left was a ballroom with the double doors opened wide. A holiday party was in full swing inside. The massive crystal chandelier that hung from the center of the frescoed ceiling had been targeted by rotating red and green gel lights in the corners of the room. The chandelier facets twinkled as if they'd been set dancing in the colors of the season. A garland of live greenery bordered the doorway with clutches of red velvet and gold glass balls at each angle and in the center. Delia looked up to find herself directly beneath a spray of mistletoe.

"That's a dangerous place to stand, young lady," a male voice said.

By the time Delia realized it wasn't Nick speaking, she had already leapt into the ballroom, out of range of those sprigs of green leaves and white berries and what they represented. She was much too unsettled by Nick to take a chance on mistletoe.

"Come on in," the man said.

That brought Delia back to her senses enough to tell her she had just crashed a private party.

"Sorry," she stammered. "I just heard the music, and—"

"There's nothing to be sorry about," the man interrupted, smiling broadly. "The more, the merrier. Please, join us."

"Oh, we couldn't do that. This is a private party, and we—"

"You can do anything I say," he interrupted again. "This is a company party, and I own the company."

He was a portly gentleman in his late fifties or sixties. From the cut of the expensive suit he was wearing, he certainly could be who he said he was. He took Delia's arm and turned back toward Nick who was standing in the doorway looking as if he might be wondering what to do next.

"Please, come along, too, young man," their self-appointed host called out to Nick. "You and your lovely companion are most welcome."

Nick hesitated. His glance moved from the man's jovial smile to Delia's face. She wasn't quite smiling, but she hoped her eyes told him how much she wanted to accept the invitation and pretend to be a normal person doing normal things, if only for a little while.

"I suppose there's no harm in it," Nick said as he took a step over the threshold.

"No harm in it?" their host exclaimed. "It's the best thing possible. There's nothing like a party to put you in the spirit of the season." He took Delia's hand and held it out to Nick. "You two have a good time. That's an order. I must be off now to take care of a few things. You help yourselves to the buffet while I'm gone."

He gestured toward the tables on either side of the doorway, laden with chafing dishes and platters brimming with food. In that instant Delia was suddenly aware of how long it had been since she'd eaten. She would have thought she was too upset to be hungry. Her stomach growled in denial of that assumption. She was ravenous. Nick must be, too, maybe even more so. A man his size needed to fortify himself regularly, but she'd kept him running so fast there'd been no opportunity to stop for a meal. She grabbed his hand even before he could take hers and began leading him toward the nearest buffet table.

"Thank you," she said, remembering her manners.

Delia turned toward their generous host, but he was scurrying off out of the double doors into the chandelier-lit foyer. He stopped and whispered something to a younger man outside the doorway who glanced back toward Delia and Nick then nodded and started toward them. Maybe this was some kind of joke or mistake and they were about to be tossed out into the gleaming parquet foyer on their ears. Delia halted her beeline for the food and wondered what should be her next move as the young man bore down on them from the doorway. Nick must have been apprehensive, as well, because he stepped between Delia and the approaching stranger but didn't let go of her hand.

"Hi, there," the young man said with such obvious good cheer that Delia couldn't help but relax. "The boss says you're his special guests and that you're under strict orders to eat, drink and be merry."

He held out his hand for Nick to shake. Delia saw Nick hesitate and sensed what must be going on in his head. Then he took the young man's hand and shook it firmly.

"My name's Rudy," the young man said. "Let me know if you need anything. There's no arguing with the boss, so you'd better have fun."

"Thanks a lot," Nick said. "We will."

Delia couldn't tell if he meant that or was just being polite. Rudy seemed to interpret it as a cue that his job was done here. He smiled and nodded before taking off into the foyer after his boss. Delia looked up at Nick. He was still holding her hand. His grip was light and warm with no insistence in it. Still, she knew she couldn't have let go no matter how hard she tried.

"I say we should take Rudy at his word," Nick said. "I could clear both of those buffet tables all by myself and have room left over for dessert."

"Me, too," Delia said.

This time, he was in the lead toward the food. She followed, wondering how she might fill her plate and still keep on holding his hand.

NICK COULDN'T remember when he'd ever been so hungry, but that wasn't why he'd decided to let them stay. Everything he knew about being a bodyguard told him they should get out of here. This was a roomful of strangers with more strangers wandering in and out at will. He'd tried to keep track of the entrance, but he didn't really know who he was watching for. Delia had described this Clyde Benno character. According to her, he was tall and blondish and pretty big. Aside from that, Nick's only clue to Benno's identity would be any suspicious behavior, such as somebody checking the room out too closely or a guy who didn't seem to belong. Of course, nobody filled that description better than Nick himself. His jeans and sweater stood out like a neon sign in this suited-up crowd. He fit here about as comfortably as a right hand in a left glove, though it was just the opposite with Delia. She'd put these dressed-to-kill women to shame anyday, no matter what she had on.

Delia was the reason Nick had made the risky decision to let them stick around here for a while. She'd been under so much strain these past couple of days that he was amazed she hadn't collapsed into exhaustion hours ago. Instead she forged on, maybe too much so. The way she'd gone darting off a while back, up and down hotel corridors, had him worried. She reminded him of a spring wound too tight and well on the road to snapping. She needed the release of being here at this party for a while. He'd have to watch her back every minute, but seeing her almost relaxed for a change was worth it. He didn't have much real choice in the matter anyway. She'd looked up at him with her eyes shining so bright they cast the crystal chandelier overhead into shadow. At that moment Nick would have done anything, gone anywhere, for her. All she had to do was ask.

Besides, he *was* starved. The thought of going back upstairs and waiting even half an hour for room service would be his idea of agony right now. He'd often marveled at how some women can go what seems like forever without eating and not show a sign of hunger. Delia'd been doing that all night, unless she had a snack stashed away in her pocket, and those jeans of hers fit a little too tight to hide much of anything. Even the jolly old guy who'd pulled them in here had noticed that. He'd checked her out up and down once at least, though without making it obvious. In fact, just about every man in this room had given her the once over. Most beautiful women lived for that kind of attention and just about glowed when they got it. Delia had a different kind of light inside her. That was how Nick would describe it, anyway, and she was all the more lovely because she didn't seem to know it was there.

He told himself he shouldn't be thinking about her this way, but he couldn't stop such thoughts of her from popping into his head every time he looked at her. He reminded himself that her direction wasn't where he should be watching. He scanned the room again. Nothing had changed. On the raised center of the floor, couples were dancing to the music spun by a DJ set up in a corner of the room. More couples and singles talked and laughed at the tables surrounding the dance floor. Nick and Delia were among the few still eating. The rest of the gathering had moved past the supper stage and were getting down to just plain enjoying themselves. Now that Nick had finished a plate of food, he could also feel the party vibes in the air. He gave himself one more reminder that he was here to do a job, not to have a good time. Sitting beside Delia made him far too susceptible to forgetting that.

"Let's dance," she said suddenly.

Nick stared at her, as if she might have been speaking an unfamiliar language.

"You know," she said. "Dancing. That's where two people get out on the floor and move around in time to the music."

The teasing tone of her voice tickled the edge of his memory, like something he'd heard before but made himself forget.

"Dance with me," she said, tugging his arm.

The teasing tone was gone, replaced by her usual insistent one. Whatever association had jogged his memory for a moment was gone now as she did her best to drag him out of his chair and he did his best to resist.

"I'm really not much of a dancer," he protested.

"Come on now. You have to be an old hand at parties like this. They're part of your job description."

"That's true." He was forever shadowing some rich client to one social event or another. "But I'm there as a watchdog, not a participant."

"Tonight's different," she said, and kept on tugging.

It sure is, Nick thought to himself. He couldn't take his eyes off the pink of her cheeks, against the ivory delicacy of the rest of her face. She was radiant. He had no will to do anything but follow that radiance up out of his chair and onto the dance floor. He was glad they were playing a fast song. He didn't trust himself to touch her right now. Chubby Checker shouted from the speakers for them to do the twist. Nick managed an approximation of that while he surveyed the other dancers on the floor and the people still at the tables. He didn't see anything unusual. He was registering that with some relief and thinking that they shouldn't stay at this party much longer, when he glanced at Delia. What he saw had him all but mesmerized in an instant.

She was dancing, but not to an amateur's stab at the beat like he was. Her hips swiveled exactly as they were supposed to for this dance, but her way of swiveling was more exotic than any version of the twist he'd ever seen. In his mind, he could hardly put together Delia Marie Barry, marching along in an uptight business suit, with the woman in front of him who moved as if the music was coming out of her bones instead of the speakers. Nick felt himself suddenly almost not breathing as her body swayed dangerously close to his. His hands itched to grab her twisting hips and pull them against him. He'd know how to twist to the music then, when he could feel her body grinding into his the way he could already feel her moving in his blood.

He was almost at the point of reaching out and doing exactly what he fantasized when the music subsided just enough to let him hear the small voice niggling at the edge of his brain. That voice said he was way out of line here, and Nick knew it was true. He tore his gaze from her body, though he needed all of his willpower to do it. The image of her breasts, round and firm beneath her sweater, remained in his vision even after he stopped looking at them. The picture faded only because of what he was finally able to register in her face.

Her expression was as absorbed by the music as her body. She looked what he could only describe as transported. Her eyes had drifted half shut as if she were gazing somewhere deep inside herself and wasn't really in this place at this moment. Her lips were parted in a way that struck Nick like a lightning bolt, straight to the stomach then downward. Her face was even more tantalizing than her body, but he wasn't thinking about looking away this time. He was remembering. He'd known only one woman who danced this way, only one other woman sensual enough to feel music in the very center of herself and be transported by it, and she had been little more than a girl at the time.

"Merry Christmas! Ho, ho, ho! Merry Christmas!"

The big, jolly voice boomed from the doorway and shot like a cannonball through Nick's tormented thoughts. Santa Claus had just burst into the ballroom with a green-clad, oversize elf in his wake. Nick commanded one hundred percent of his attention back to the present, and gradually his senses obeyed. Nothing activated his natural suspiciousness like people in costumes. He stepped in front of Delia as the crowd parted to make way for Santa and his helper to get to the center of the room. Santa was carrying a very large sack. He could have anything in there, up to and including an AK-47. Nick reached behind him and grabbed Delia's arm so he could pull her closer and know exactly where she was. The music had changed from rock and roll to "Santa Claus Is Coming To Town," but Nick wasn't really listening. He was too busy trying to watch Santa and the rest of the people in the room while sidling himself and Delia away from the center of the crowd around the fat man in the red suit.

"It's him," Delia exclaimed as she pulled against Nick and back toward the center of the dance floor.

"Where?"

Nick's free hand went automatically to the back of his waistband. His first thought was that she'd spotted Clyde Benno. Nick never drew his gun in a crowded place if he could help it, but he was ready all the same.

"Right there," she said. She didn't sound scared, only excited. "Santa Claus is the man who said he owned this company, and Rudy's playing his elf." She laughed in a peal that sounded like holiday bells. "Look, Nick." She tugged his arm. "Rudy's painted his nose red. Get it? Rudolf the Red-Nosed Reindeer? Except he's Rudy the Red-Nosed Elf."

Nick stared at Santa, then at his elf, then at Delia who had pulled out from behind him. She had a smile on her face as wide and full of joy as a kid on Christmas morning. Nick did get it then. He heaved a sigh of relief and let himself relax a little, though he still kept a sharp watch as Rudy held the bag open and Santa pulled out packages. Gifts wrapped in red went to the men, and the ones wrapped in gold were for the women. Nick tried to hold Delia back, then gave up and went along as she followed the throng toward Santa who was ho-hoing up a storm and obviously enjoying his role.

"Merry Christmas, young lady," he chortled merrily as he handed Delia her gold package.

"Thank you, Santa," she piped as she planted a kiss on his ruddy cheek.

Santa colored even ruddier. "Thank you, my dear," he said, and pressed a red-wrapped parcel into Nick's hand without really looking at him.

She even captivates Saint Nick, he thought, suddenly aware that he had the same name as this chubby old figure. Delia was opening her gift in the meantime, as if she could hardly wait to see what Santa had left under the tree. Nick felt her childlike eagerness with a pang that caught in his throat. Suddenly he understood something about her that hadn't come clear till this moment. She was lonely. At the same instant he admitted something about himself, as well, more pointedly than he'd ever done. He was lonely, too. Out of that awareness his heart reached for hers.

He would have taken her in his arms right then, but she had stepped away from him. The gold ribbon and wrapping were off her package now, floating forgotten to the dance floor as she stared at what she was holding in her hand—a gold pasteboard box with the top removed. All Nick could make out was the fringe of white tissue paper she had pulled aside to reveal the box's contents. He was pushing past people to get to her side when he heard the sound she made, somewhere between a cry and a moan. Then she was running toward the double doors. As Nick headed after her, someone took his arm.

"Is something wrong?" Rudy asked, looking concerned.

"I don't know."

Nick moved to pull away, but Rudy didn't let go.

"Is she sick? Should I call the house doctor?"

Rudy was obviously in charge of putting things right in Santa's kingdom, and he was persistent at doing his job. Nick shook his arm off all the same.

"She had to go to the ladies' room," he said for want of a better excuse. He had to be after Delia before she could get very far away. Still, he didn't want Rudy to follow them. Delia was a client first and foremost. That meant Nick's job was to shield her from prying eyes, no matter how well intentioned they might be. "We have to be leaving now. Thanks for everything."

Nick forced himself to stay calm and avoid attracting further attention as he moved purposefully toward the door. He barely heard the "Ho, ho, ho," still booming from the center of the ballroom.

Chapter Ten

Delia clutched the small, gold box to her chest and kept her tears from falling. All she could think of was getting to her room where she could be alone and let the feelings come tumbling out. She didn't dare look again at the contents of the box. She didn't dare even think about those contents. If she did that, she'd be lost. The tears and the memories would be unleashed and stopping them would no longer be possible. She must make it to the sanctuary of her room before she could allow that to happen.

Fortunately, there was nobody in the foyer to see her scrambling exit from the ballroom. They were all back inside, clustered around Santa or opening their gifts. Even Nick hadn't yet followed her out of there. She knew she should wait for him to catch up, but she simply had to make her escape.

She glanced up at the parade of chandeliers on the ceiling of the wide corridor leading away from the ballroom. Potted palms lined the mirrored walls. The ceiling was high, arched and vaulted, with paintings like those in the ballroom. The black and white squares of tiled floor reflected the glittering chandeliers. This was one of the most elegant places Delia had ever seen, more of a showcase than a place to hide.

She turned right, back up the stairway that had first led her and Nick to the party in the ballroom. Those stairs felt steeper and appeared to be at least twice as numerous as they had when she was hurrying down them toward sounds of holiday merriment. She could hardly wait to get away from that merriment now. She was climbing so hastily her foot slipped on the carpeted step and she had to grab the handrail to steady herself. She kept a tight grip on that rail as she continued to climb. Otherwise she might have lost her balance straight off when the man lunged at her.

She hadn't noticed him coming up the stairs behind her. She'd been too deeply immersed in the welter of her thoughts to notice much of anything. Suddenly, as if out of nowhere, he was bearing down on her. She recognized him instantly as the same man who'd chased her through Rockefeller Plaza the other night. She'd seen his face more clearly than she realized at the time. The face looming over her was unmistakably the same, except for the eyes that were far more frightening than could have been detected at a distance. He'd seemed ordinary in appearance then, though taller than average. She could see now that his eyes were also anything but average. They were wide open and round and staring with something not quite sane at their center. She knew for certain that she'd never seen him before the other night, and that made him even more terrifying somehow.

"You won't get away this time," he said.

His voice was pitched low, but he couldn't have been more menacing if he'd shouted. The corners of his mouth turned up in a parody of a smile. That, along with the eyes, gave him a maniacal look that made Delia want to turn and run back down the stairs. Unfortunately she couldn't manage that without letting go of the handrail. Instinct told her he was hoping she'd do just that. Then he'd push her backward, down onto the hard parquet floor at the bottom of the stairs. She held her ground and her grip on the rail. She didn't let go of the gold box, either. She wouldn't relinquish her precious gift without a fight. Instead she lifted the box in a menacing movement of her own.

"Get out of my way," she said.

She was surprised by the strength of her voice considering that she could feel her legs trembling beneath her. His lunatic stare moved from her face to her raised hand and lingered there a moment, as if he couldn't believe she was nervy enough to try threatening him with a flimsy, pasteboard box.

"I told you to get out of my way," she repeated even more firmly.

He returned his glance to her face and chuckled. He didn't move away as she'd commanded. He leaned closer and unwittingly gave her the opportunity she needed. At this angle he was slightly off balance. She saw that and launched her attack. The open box descended. It might have appeared a futile missile except that she knew what was inside, still exposed between the sheaves of tissue paper she hadn't taken time to rewrap when she'd hurried from the ballroom.

The edge of the object in the box caught him, as she'd hoped it would, just below the temple. The red blood was so quick to appear there that Delia was startled by it, but not sufficiently startled to miss her chance. He teetered on the stair just long enough for her to let go of the rail and push, hard as she could at his chest. He had one hand up to touch the wound on his forehead. Maybe that was what kept him from maintaining his stance. He staggered toward the opposite wall of the stairwell.

She brushed past him, retrieved the box and bolted up the stairs, fully expecting him to grab her arm or even her ankle at any moment. She'd let go of the handrail. Hanging on would have slowed her down so she took the risk of letting go. The smooth soles of her boots slid precariously over the carpeting. She pushed on, leaning forward both to propel herself in that direction and to keep from falling backward down the stairs. With each step, she was certain he would overtake her and was astonished that he didn't. Then she heard the reason why—the sounds of muttered oaths and scuffling.

Delia reached the top of the stairs. She turned to see the man and Nick grappling halfway up the flight. She hesitated just as Nick glanced in her direction. "Run," he shouted in a tone so urgent and demanding she almost didn't recognize it as his. That tone plus her own common sense told her she should obey. She did exactly that. She ran down the corridor away from the stairs and didn't look back.

WHEN HE SAW the guy after Delia, Nick just about went out of his head. He sprinted up the stairs two at a time and grabbed the guy by the shoulders. She'd already done some damage. Blood ran down his forehead into his eyebrow. Nick was proud of her for that. She knew how to stand up for herself. Now he'd finish the job. He shoved the guy so hard up against the wall the mirrors rattled above them.

"Leave her alone," Nick growled. "Stop following her around."

He punctuated his words by slamming the guy against the wall again. He grunted in reply. He was a weaselly looking character. Nick couldn't imagine beautiful, accomplished Delia with somebody like this. She really had him going, all right. His eyes blazed out of his face. Still, Nick didn't feel sympathy for this guy any longer. No matter what she'd done to him, he had no right to make her life miserable. He especially didn't have a right to try to hurt her. Nick slammed him again, and the guy's head lolled on his neck like a rag doll.

"You come near her again, and I'll kill you."

Nick was shocked by how strongly he meant those words. He wasn't a killer by nature.

"No, buddy," the guy said in a cracked voice, his eyes glittering like burning coals. "I'll kill you."

Nick sensed the gun before he saw or felt it. This guy might have eyes that were on fire, but Nick had some rage of his own to vent right now. This creep was trying to hurt Delia, and Nick wasn't about to stand for that. His reaction was lightning swift, faster even than a trigger finger and far less expected. He raised his arm and drove his elbow into the guy's throat in a single, powerful motion. The blazing eyes went blank for an instant. In that flash, Nick grabbed the guy's gun arm and twisted till the weapon dropped free. Nick yanked him away from the wall, turned him toward the descending stairwell and pushed. The man toppled backward, arms flailing, down the stairs, grunting and cursing till he hit the parquet floor where he lay crumpled and quiet. Nick followed down the stairs. The guy was knocked out but still breathing. Nick knew he didn't have to shove the guy down the stairs like that, but he'd needed a lesson he wouldn't forget. Now, Nick had to make himself scarce before security showed up and brought this mess back to Delia's doorstep in a way she wouldn't like.

The gun had bounced down the stairs and was lying next to its owner. Nick picked it up. The thought that this creep came here after Delia with a gun on him had Nick white-hot again until he looked down at the weapon in his hand. It was a 9 mm Beretta. Something about that very serious weapon and the look of the guy in general clicked a recognition switch in Nick's head. He'd been too angry to put it together before. His cop's instinct was usually with him every minute, but he'd let himself get emotionally involved here. That could screw anybody up. His instinct was back on course now, and it was telling him something very disturbing. This guy on the floor wasn't just some flake from Long Island. He was a pro.

Nick would have liked to toss the guy's pockets right here, but he didn't have time. Somebody was bound to come out of the ballroom any minute. There'd be trouble for sure then, and that wouldn't be good for Delia. If all they found was this guy passed out on the floor, they'd figure he drank too much and fell. If what Nick suspected about this guy was true, he'd most likely go along with that story. He wouldn't want hotel security in on this any more than Nick did. On the other hand, if somebody came out here and found Nick standing over this dude, there'd be alarm bells going off all over the place.

Nick pocketed the Beretta and headed back up the stairs. He picked up the gift package he'd dropped before grabbing the guy. No need to leave any traces behind. Nick pulled absently at the red wrapping paper as he hurried down the hallway toward the corridor that would take him out of sight of the stairwell and in the direction of the elevators. Alarm bells of his own were clanging in his brain to beat the band. Had Delia been stupid enough to let herself get mixed up with a professional gunman? Everything Nick had ever learned in this business told him that didn't ring true.

Loose ends of her story that he hadn't paid enough attention to before were suddenly dangling right in front of him. There was definitely something off-line with what she'd told him. He could see that now plain as day. He was used to being lied to. Clients lied all the time, even when their lies made it more difficult to keep them protected. He'd expected more than that from Delia, and not just because she was in the business herself and should know better. He'd expected more because of what he'd started feeling for her. "Emotions cloud judgment." If that bodyguard manual of his had a first-of-all rule, this was it. He'd forgotten his own first rule. Nick told himself he wouldn't forget it again.

By the time he reached the elevators, he'd torn the wrapping off the gift box and opened it without even realizing what he was doing. He glanced down at the box while he waited impatiently for an up arrow to flash red above one of the elevator doors. The tissue paper had been pushed aside to reveal a necktie in very proper regimental striped design except for the Santa face in the center. Nick pulled the tie out and put the box down beside a vase of flowers on a table next to the elevator bank. He ran the length of silky fabric between his fingers. He couldn't help wondering who should be strangled with this thing—the professional hitter back there laid out on the floor or Nick's own lying client.

Nick spent the rest of the trip to his room calming himself down and doing some thinking. When he raised his fist to knock on the adjoining door to Delia's room, he had more than one big question on his mind. It took a couple of knocks to get an answer.

"Who is it?" she asked from the other side of the door.

"It's Nick," he said, subdued a little by what sounded like fear in her voice. "Are you okay?"

"I'm fine," she said, though he could hear that wasn't true. "But I'm not up to talking right now."

Nick could feel the tremor in her voice melting his resolve. Tremor or not, there was one thing he had to find out. He leaned close to the door panel so he wouldn't have to talk loud.

"How did that guy know we were here?"

She was silent for a moment before she answered. "I did something very dumb."

"What was that?"

Another pause. "I left the hotel phone number with my office answering service. I always let them know where I'm going to be. He must have called and found out where I was, then waited down in the lobby till we showed up."

Nick sighed and shook his head.

"Can we please talk about this later?"

She was pleading now. That, plus the thought of her being so conscientious about her job that she put herself in danger, deflated his anger faster than he would have guessed was possible.

"Sure," he said. "Get some sleep. We'll talk tomorrow."

"Thanks," she said, her voice smaller than ever. "Good night."

"Good night."

Nick stared at her door for a moment longer. He had yet another question. Wasn't she just a little too devoted to that job of hers? Or was he just being overly suspicious to make up for not being suspicious enough before? Whatever his reasons, he was determined to get the answers to all of his questions in the morning. He could use some sleep himself. But, with the way he had the Santa necktie clutched into a tight ball in his fist, he wasn't likely to find much sleep on his agenda tonight.

DELIA WAS DREAMING when the sound began, trying to get her feet off the ground to fly. Then the jangling started and the dream dissolved. What was going on? What was this noise, and where was she, anyway?

The last answer came first. She was in a hotel. That's why she didn't know where anything was. She groped off the side of the bed where the table lamp should be and found empty space. The darkness in the room was total. She'd drawn the blackout drapes before going to bed. Now she wished she'd left them open for the light from the street to come through. She'd be able to get her bearings if she could see something. Her hand hit the smooth, china surface of what had to be the hotel bedside lamp. She felt upward over the curved surface but found no switch. She ran her hand back down to the bottom of the lamp and around the circular metal base, still feeling for a switch.

Meanwhile the sound continued, more of a buzz than the jangling it had first seemed to be. She'd figured out that the buzz must be from an alarm clock. She was trying to piece together why she'd set the alarm when her fingers hit the light switch. She twisted it, and the room filled with light. All she saw was the clock radio on the other side of the lamp. She grabbed it and poked the buttons on top till the buzzing stopped as abruptly as it had begun.

Two hours had passed since she'd drifted into an uneasy sleep. She wasn't yet entirely awake. She was still caught at the edge of dreaming when another real world sound reached her ears, softer and less jarring than the alarm buzzer had been. Delia drifted up from the bed and followed the knocking sound to the door between her room and Nick Avery's. This time she would open that door.

Chapter Eleven

Nick heard Delia disengage the lock on her side of the door. He'd recognized the alarm clock sound and wondered why she would have set it for the middle of the night. As her bodyguard, he needed to know the answer to that, especially if she planned to leave her room on her own for any reason with that tall, blond guy from last night still on the loose. Besides, Nick had been sleeping only fitfully himself.

There was silence after the door clicked.

"Delia?" Nick called. "Are you there?"

The silence continued for a moment before she answered.

"I'm here, Nick." Her voice was faint but unmistakable.

"Are you all right?" he asked.

No answer again. Maybe something was wrong. Could the tall man have gotten to her somehow? Could she be his prisoner? If that was true, he'd be using her as a shield. Nick slipped to his bedstand, grabbed his gun and checked the clip before returning to the doorway. He took hold of the doorknob just as it was turning in his hand. That made him think caution, but he moved rapidly like a spring suddenly released. In a lightning-quick snap he had yanked the door open and stood at an angle in the opening. What he saw made him relax in one way and tense further in another.

Her eyes looked almost as if she might still be asleep. They were heavy-lidded, gazing at him with a curious expression, as if she couldn't quite remember who he might be. She wasn't entirely awake, though she'd put on a robe. That must have been what kept her from opening the door right away. Her nightgown was visible underneath her partly opened robe. The gown was made of white cotton and hung long enough to touch the floor beneath the hem of her robe. The garments were loose rather than formfitting. They might as well have been slinky, transparent and halfway up her thighs. Nick saw her as maddeningly sexy, anyway.

He had just about enough sense left to note that there was nobody but her in the room. The louvered closet door was open across from him, and he could tell no one was hiding inside. They were alone. He should have made one more visual survey of the room—checked under the bed and in the bathroom—but her face told him everything the professional part of him needed to know. If somebody had broken in here and surprised her while she was sleeping, her eyes would be startled, not dreamy. He could see just a hint of apprehension there, but instinct told him that wasn't because someone was lurking in the bathroom.

Every guideline of businesslike behavior, including the ones in his own head, insisted Nick should turn directly around right now and go back to his own room. Instead he pulled the connecting door closed behind him and flipped the latch to locked position. The flicker of apprehension in her eyes intensified a little then, but she didn't move. She held her ground with her full lips slightly parted as if she might be about to say something. He could hear her soft breath coming faster than before.

Nick couldn't stand it any longer. He whispered her name. Then he was across the space between them and she was in his arms, pressed against him where he so very much needed her to be. He'd been sleeping in just a T-shirt when the sound from this room awakened him. He'd pulled on his jeans, and he could feel her now through the denim. She was warm even though the room had cooled from its earlier temperature. Or was that his own heat he was feeling?

He knew he was hard as a rock inside his jeans. He'd been that way from the first instant he saw her. He pressed that hardness against her. He wanted her to feel how much he wanted her. She moaned softly. She'd felt it, and she wasn't moving away. She wanted him, too. He didn't let himself think that maybe it wasn't really him she wanted, maybe she was just lonely. He didn't let himself think about anything. In fact, the last thing his sensible mind registered was that he still had his gun in his hand, and he didn't want it to be there.

He was looking for a place to lay his weapon down when Delia slid her hand down his arm behind her back and took hold of the gun. He maintained his grip for a moment. That much instinct was left in his besotted brain—to resist having his weapon taken from him, but not for long. His fingers loosened, and he let her ease the pistol from his grasp. She stepped back out of his arms and held the gun in both hands for a moment. She seemed to be caressing it, or maybe Nick just saw it that way. He felt that caress as if her hands were on the most intimate part of his body. He wouldn't have thought he could get any harder there, but he did now.

He heard her put the gun down on top of the credenza next to the ice bucket and glasses, yet he only half realized her hands were empty again as he lifted her in his arms and carried her toward the bed. Suddenly she was clasping him around the neck and had buried her head against his shoulder. Her hair brushed his face. The sweet scent of those sleek locks was overwhelming. He might have staggered, but he was too intent upon getting her to the bed to lose even a second from faltering along the way.

He lay her down gently on the rumpled sheet with her head on the pillow. He straightened to almost his full height and looked down at her. His own lips were parted now, and he could hear his ragged breathing. He had never seen anything anywhere near as beautiful as her hair, fallen against the white pillowcase. He longed to leap on top of her and crush her to the bed with his body, but he also longed to make the exquisite ache of looking at her last.

Nick's gaze traveled slowly over her, pausing to take in the most breathtaking details. Her lips were so full and reddened, they begged to be kissed. He hadn't kissed her yet, other than a thousand times in his imagination. He would kiss her soon now. That thought made him pull his T-shirt over his head and toss it onto the floor. His gaze moved along her creamy throat to the soft heaving of her breasts. He opened the button at the waistband of his jeans and took hold of the metal tab. His gaze moved downward over her as his fingers pushed his zipper in the same direction. The zipper resisted moving over the hard mound beneath, but her body didn't resist his eyes. She moved—just a little—a slight roll of her hips toward him. There could have been no more sultry invitation as far as Nick was concerned. His breath turned rapid as well as ragged.

She pulled the tie loose on her robe and let it fall open. The delicate cotton of her gown molded her body and was nearly transparent in the soft light. His gaze rested on a shadow of darkness between her thighs. She wasn't wearing panties. She was totally nude beneath her gown, and waiting for him. Nick shoved his zipper the rest of the way down. He wasn't wearing underwear, either. He pushed his jeans down over his hips and felt himself spring free—harder and longer and maybe even more menacing than the barrel of his gun had been. But he didn't plan to use this or any other part of himself as a weapon, only as an instrument of pleasure.

He saw her gaze travel down his body. Her eyes widened when they reached his loins. Her full lips moved lazily into a smile. Her hips rolled again, even more obviously inviting this time. Nick swallowed but couldn't really catch his breath. He slid his jeans down more and pulled his right leg free of them. He was almost crazily overjoyed that he hadn't put on socks or shoes. He pulled the other leg out of his jeans without taking his eyes off of her, but he didn't stumble. His rational mind might be on another planet, but the rest of him was right here and steady on course toward taking this woman as he had never taken a woman before.

Her hand had been at her side. She drew it across her body, letting her fingers barely touch herself, over the gentle rise of her belly, upward to her breast and over the swelling there, very slowly, to her nipple, which was visibly taut beneath the delicate cloth. Her lips were still parted, and her breath was still in what he could hear was the rhythm of desire. She was tantalizing him, and she was tantalizing herself at the same time. She had picked up on his determination to take this at a certain pace, to torture every delicious moment till they both felt about to explode. Then to go on and do the same thing with the next moment.

Her fingers trailed around her nipple in a circle that nearly killed him as surely as if she had shot at him with his gun. He could see the point of her tongue just behind her parted lips, beckoning him to put his own tongue there, just as her circling fingers were beckoning him to her breast. His mesmerized senses flashed on an image of another part of her, as pink and moist as the tip of her tongue. His own fingers and tongue and then the hard evidence of his wanting her, now thrusting straight out from his body, would claim that part of her, too.

Her fingers left their circling path and continued up to the lacy strap of her gown where the robe had slipped from her silky shoulder. She was about to push that strap aside, but Nick said, "No. Let me do that. Let me do everything." And she did.

IT WAS HOURS later before they finally slept. In the morning, Delia awoke first. This time she had no doubt about where she was or about the difference between reality and dream. Last night, her reality had been a dream. She could feel the man at the center of that dream still asleep at her side. His warmth added to her own beneath the sheet and blanket, like a cozy nest against the winter cold. She could hear him, too. The soft cadence of his breathing was proof to her that their lovemaking actually had happened, no matter how impossible its beauty might seem. No gift could be more precious than that, and she thanked her Christmas angel for it.

That thought made her reach toward the bedside table. Last night, after hurrying back from the ghastly scene on the ballroom stairway, she'd left the gold gift box on the table. She touched the edges of the object still nestled among its tissue wrappings—a crystal angel with a golden cord suspended from its halo for hanging in a window or from a tree limb. This little angel had been more than a decoration last night. This angel had been her guardian in a crystal clear way, literally arming her to ward off danger, just as years ago her father had said a very similar glass angel would protect her from harm. It was that special gift she'd remembered when she'd first opened this box. A single glimpse inside brought with it a shock of memory that had sent her running from the ballroom. She'd left that other glass angel behind five years ago in her haste to escape Colorado. She'd regretted its loss ever since. This new angel felt like a restoration of some of that loss, all tied together in her heart with the man who lay next to her now.

Suddenly, feeling and hearing him were not enough. Delia needed to see him, too. She rolled slowly toward her edge of the bed, being careful not to pull the covers from his body. She didn't want him to wake up just yet. She sat up on the side of the bed and listened. His breathing remained steady, undisturbed. She slid from beneath the covers and stood. The cooler air of the room chilled her skin, but she didn't search for her robe. Moving around to do that would be too likely to make noise. She tiptoed naked to the window instead and felt for the edge of the blackout curtain. She pushed the opaque drapery back from first one side of the window then the other, taking care to slide them silently along the track above.

She was shivering as she crept to the bed. She would have liked to dive under the covers to get to their warmth as fast as she could. She restrained herself from that and slipped slowly between the sheets. Her attentiveness was rewarded by the unbroken rhythm of Nick's breathing. He was still asleep. She longed to burrow her icy toes beneath the toasty shelter of his body, but that would surely wake him and not gently, either. Delia pulled the sheet and blanket up to her chin and turned her face toward his on the pillow. His arm was flung across his eyes while the morning light fell lovingly on the rest of his face. She knew it might not sound manly as a description, but to her in that moment he was entirely beautiful. In that moment, also, she knew what she must do. She must tell Nick the whole truth, no matter what the consequences.

NICK FELT HER there even before he opened his eyes— not her exactly, but the soft brush of her hair against his chest. In any other circumstance he would have bolted straight up off the pillow the instant someone touched him in his sleep. He'd probably also make that move with a weapon in his hand, but he wasn't about to do that now. First of all, for once, he'd gone to sleep without a firearm under his pillow. He'd had things other than guns on his mind last night. For once, he'd allowed himself to be a man ahead of being a professional. Of course, he'd noticed the safety lock was on the door when he came into Delia's room. He wasn't about to put her in danger, after all. Still, he'd come to bed without packing iron so he had no weapon to brandish now, even if he'd wanted to.

And he did not need one. His immediate immersion in Delia's presence let him know that, all the way to the very center of himself. His first waking awareness was of her being with him. The scent of her enveloped him like the fragrant breath of soft wings fluttering. He could feel the coolness of her skin even without touching her. The impression of her face was on the inside of his eyelids long before they eased open to that same face, lovelier still than in his imaginings. At first he didn't think to wonder why she wasn't smiling, why her extraordinary eyes held such a serious expression. He needed a full waking moment before that question could form in his mind.

"Good morning," she said.

The melody of her voice might have banished all notion of questioning anything about her if it hadn't been for the melancholy edge to that melody. Something was wrong. He could hear it. He could see it. Still, he wanted it not to be true. In that moment he wished with his entire heart to be mistaken and for everything to remain perfect—as it had been last night and should be now.

"Nick," she said. "I have something to tell you."

Here it comes, he thought. His first impulse was to clamp his hands over his ears, or maybe over her sweet mouth, before the words that he sensed would shatter everything could be spoken.

"Do we have to talk now? Can't it wait?" he asked.

Nick ordinarily prided himself in meeting every challenge straight-on, whatever it might be. Nevertheless, right now he didn't fault himself for his squeamishness. Other qualities than boldness were important here. Delia only shook her head in answer, but with that small movement she sealed their fate. Nick was sure of it. He might even have an inkling of what she was about to say—a premonition, or maybe even a sure knowledge, hidden by a mist just above the surface of his thoughts. He had the feeling that all he would have to do was press a little harder at his memory and he would know her crucial news on his own. She spoke before he could apply that effort.

"My name isn't really Delia Marie Barry," she said. "At least, that's not the name I was born with."

Nick's mouth opened, as if to finish what she was saying, though his conscious mind had no idea how he would do that.

"We've known each other before," she continued. A tear had formed in the corner of each of her lovely eyes. "My real name is Becky Lester."

Nick gasped, but it came out sounding more like a groan. One of her trembling tears fell onto his chest before she could duck her head and hide her face. He would have liked to lift her chin and wipe the tears from her eyes. He would have liked to tell her she didn't need to cry because everything would be all right. He couldn't do that because it wouldn't be the truth.

"Rebecca," he breathed.

It never occurred to Nick to doubt her words. The instant she spoke them, he'd felt things slide together like the pieces of a puzzle. Dangling elements—things she'd told him, things she hadn't told him, hints of a connection he hadn't quite grasped before—wove themselves into a discernable pattern at last.

"Why?" he asked. It was all he could do to think clearly enough to talk.

She continued to hang her head, shaking it every moment or so as if in a daze.

"I had to tell you the truth," she said, her words muffled by the hair screening her face.

She'd answered another question that would have come later, but not the one he was asking now.

"Why did you lie to me?" he asked. "Why didn't you tell me the whole story from the start?"

Nick had to fight to keep his voice from quavering, like her tears, which were dropping, sad seconds apart, from her averted eyes.

"I didn't dare tell you the truth," she said.

"Why not?" He did take her chin and lift her face now. He swallowed against the heartache he saw there. He mustn't weaken before he had his answer. "Why couldn't you tell me?"

She sighed so deeply he could feel the tremor of it across the space between their bodies.

"I wasn't sure I could trust you," she said.

"What did you think I'd do?" He was still holding her chin so she couldn't look away.

"You might have called the police...." She trailed off into another sigh.

"You believe I could have done that?"

"I couldn't be altogether sure. What happened five years ago taught me not to be sure of anybody."

The way she said that—all defiance gone now, only a near-sob left—reminded him of back in the ballroom, when he'd recognized how lonely she was. Nothing could be lonelier than living without trust, afraid to let anyone close enough to become a threat. He could imagine the poignancy of that life because he'd lived some of it himself, though never as completely or with the degree of desolation that had been her fate. Nick's anger melted away, maybe not forever but for now. He reached out and folded her—Delia, Becky, Rebecca, whoever she might be—into the comfort of his arms.

Chapter Twelve

Delia clung to Nick for what felt like a very long time but not nearly long enough. She would have wanted to make love again. Making love with Nick was being swept away on a wave of emotion deeper and wider than anything she'd ever known. She could let that wave take her. She could give up thinking about what was going to happen next and what she should do about it and simply be borne away, higher and farther than anyone's touch had ever taken her before. She could use that kind of release right now. She longed for it. She even sensed that Nick might feel the same, but neither of them made a move. They'd been through so much in these past hours together, they needed to be still for a while. His arms cradled her body. Her arms circled his neck. They were safe here for the moment in the silence. Delia knew that couldn't last. Unfortunately, there was more to be talked about. When the next question came, she'd already told herself she had to be ready for it.

"What about Clyde Benno?" Nick asked. "Have you told me the whole story on him?"

Nick kept his arms around her. There was no anger or bitterness in his voice. Still, she could feel the chill wind of the inevitable in his words, and that made her sigh.

"There is no Clyde Benno. I made him up."

She was amazed at how easy it was to let that cat finally out of the bag and at how relieved she was to watch it scamper away, beyond her control. In the meantime, Nick only nodded and continued to hold her.

"You don't seem surprised," she said.

"I spotted that guy last night for a professional. I didn't think you'd have a thug for a boyfriend, not even one who knows how to pass as respectable. I didn't think an angry ex-boyfriend would hire a guy like that, either. Usually, angry ex-boyfriends prefer to do the dirty work themselves. They get more satisfaction that way."

It was Delia's turn to nod. "That sounds right to me," she said.

"The thing that almost threw me off was his eyes. That part of him looked like he could be the psycho boyfriend after all."

Delia remembered those eyes much too clearly. She doubted she'd ever forget them. She shivered, and Nick folded her closer to the broad, hard safety of his chest. She nestled there gladly.

"Those eyes could be the key to tracking him down," Nick said. "Either he really is crazy or he's taking something that makes him look that way. My guess is one or the other's got him noticed. Maybe if I ask the right people the right questions, I could find out who he is. That would put us closer to finding out who hired him."

"I know who hired him."

"You do?"

Nick thrust her away from him when he asked that, so he could look into her face. She nearly sighed again. She was being pushed out of the warm circle of his arms. It might be a long time before she nestled there again.

"I don't know the specific identity of the person who did the hiring," she said, resigning herself to getting back to business. "But I'm almost a hundred percent sure what they're after."

"What are they after?"

"The Lester money, and they have to make sure I'm out of the way for real and for good to get it, just like they got rid of poor Morty Lancer."

Delia pulled her robe from the bottom of the bed and put it on. She was all the way out of his arms now. She felt a lonely pang of regret.

"Have you ruled out other possibilities, like somebody connected with PEI? The company could have angered a lot of people over the years, and you're the most visible target."

I'm the only target, she thought. I'm the company.

She wasn't ready to tell him that part yet. One major revelation at a time was all she could manage right now.

"I know this hasn't got anything to do with the company," she said.

"How do you know that?"

By the angle of the hair standing up on the back of my neck, was what she almost answered. She decided to be less abrupt than that. She knotted the tie of her robe then turned fully toward him.

"I've been living with running away for a long time," she said. She made sure her voice didn't plead for sympathy. She just wanted to explain how it was for her. "I've developed a kind of added sense that most people don't have. That sense lets me know who I should watch out for and why. Right now it's letting me know my past has finally caught up with me.''

"I see.''

This time his saying that didn't bother her. "I imagine you do. You must have your own radar for trouble to be as good as you are at what you do.''

"That's how I knew that guy last night was somebody more than just Clyde Benno from Long Island.''

"I'm sorry about lying to you,'' she said. "I've been living a lie for so long now. Sometimes I think it's more natural for me to make up things than to tell the truth.''

"You're good at it. I can vouch for that.''

Delia felt herself blush.

"I want to be nothing but honest with you from now on,'' she said.

"Then tell me why you left Colorado the way you did.''

"The cards were stacked against me, that's why. I'd have been charged with Morty's murder for sure, and very possibly convicted of it, too.''

"I would have helped you.''

"Oh, Nick,'' she sighed. "What could you have done? Other than maybe destroy some of the evidence against me. I knew you were too straightforward for that.'' She touched his cheek gently. "I want to be just as straight with you from this moment on.''

Nick put his fingers gently against her lips. "There'll be time for promises later,'' he said.

Delia nodded. "Okay.''

She prayed he was right. With somebody out to kill her, and maybe Nick, too, there might not be a "later'' for them, after all.

"WHAT DO YOU WANT me to call you?" Nick asked. "Delia or Becky?"

They'd decided to leave the Waldorf. The pro who was after them might not have their room numbers yet, but it was only a matter of time till he did. Nick had told Delia to throw her few belongings back in her bag, and they'd left the five-star life behind by the back entrance taxi port. Nick kept himself from thinking about how much he'd rather stay holed up in that hotel room making love to her forever. That was just one of the thoughts about her he couldn't get into, at least not till she was out of danger.

"Call me Delia," she said after a long moment when she must have been considering her answer carefully. "Becky was five years ago. Delia is now. They're not the same woman."

Nick looked across the cab seat at her, while memory overlapped what he saw. She was right. Delia and Becky were very different from one another. He wondered how deep those differences ran and what they meant to what had happened in Delia's bed last night. That was something else he couldn't let himself be sidetracked into thinking about right now. He forced himself to stop looking at her and turned toward the window. Her beautiful face and how much it was coming to mean to him was the biggest distraction of all. He had trouble keeping his head clear when he was looking at her. His head needed to be clear as glass if he was going to keep her safe. He resolved to make that kind of clarity his first and foremost priority. They rode the rest of the few blocks from the Waldorf to the Lincoln Building in silence.

EMPLOYING a private mail service was another one of Delia's hedges against detection. Not even the company letterhead carried the actual address of her Rockefeller Center office. All mail went to her mail service in the Lincoln Building on 42nd Street. She left Nick in the cab, behind the Lincoln on 41st, while she went to the eleventh floor. He'd wanted to come with her, but she insisted she'd be only a moment and hopped out into the street. She'd disappeared around the corner before he could have time enough to pay the fare and follow. She trusted him for the most part. After last night, maybe she even trusted him altogether. Still, she went to the mail service office by herself. This same company handled her telephone messages as well as her mail, and she wanted to explain her present confused situation in person. They could forward calls to her Rock Center number or take messages. She'd call in regularly for those messages, but they wouldn't be able to contact her directly except at her office. The pleasant woman in the back office wrote down Delia's instructions but asked no questions. They were discreet, which was part of the reason Delia used their services.

She left the eleventh floor office with a plastic bagful of what looked like mostly bills and junk mail, except for one piece. It was square and sturdy, as if whatever might be inside was made of card stock rather than regular stationery-weight paper. Delia examined that envelope warily. This was the season for sending and receiving holiday cards. Most people would not have taken so much notice of such an envelope. Most people would have lots of friends and relatives sending them greetings of the seasons. Delia, on the other hand, had no such circle of acquaintance. She hadn't received a Christmas card, other than corporate greet-

ings from business associates, in five years. This
envelope was handwritten and didn't look like a corporate mailing.

Delia thrust her trembling index finger under the envelope flap and tore it open, leaving a ragged edge.
She'd been right. There was a card in the envelope, on
green card stock with a snow-covered country scene on
the front. She flipped the card open and let her eyes
slide past the printed greeting to the signature. She
didn't gasp. She simply stopped breathing and stood,
still and transfixed as that snow-covered scene, just
around the corner from the elevator bank, in the middle of the beige marble hallway on the eleventh floor of
the Lincoln Building. There were three words handwritten on the bottom of the inside flap of the otherwise ordinary Christmas acknowledgment she held in
her shaking hand. Those three words made this card
about as out of the ordinary as it could be.

Those three words were, "Merry Christmas, Topsy."

Delia's mouth had dropped open. Fortunately, the
hallway was deserted. She would surely have attracted
attention if there was anyone around to see her, standing so obviously aghast as she was. The last thing Delia
wanted right now was attention. She would have liked
to sit down, but the hallway was as empty of furniture
as it was of people. Her legs were unsteady under her.
If they became any more so, she might have to sit on the
floor before she fell there. Still, she made no effort to
compose herself. She had neither will nor presence of
mind to make such an attempt right now. She was too
riveted on those three scribbled words and beyond them
to the associations they made for her. Only one person
in her entire life had ever called her Topsy. It was a

nickname that nobody else knew about. That person was her father.

Delia shut her mouth and swallowed the sob that threatened to rise from her throat. She was only barely conscious of the dryness of that swallow as she forced herself to think once more. She stared at the handwriting on the card and tried to remember her father's penmanship, but her mind moved slowly still. She seemed to recall his handwriting being close to a scrawl, like the writing on the card. It had been so long since she'd seen anything written by him. Besides, she'd made a point of putting the details of her former life as far from her present thinking as she could push them. Now she found that retrieving those details was difficult. Still, one unforgettable truth remained. Her father had pledged never to reveal her secret nickname, and he never had. She was certain of it. Or maybe she only wanted to be certain of it because that would mean the most impossible of Christmas miracles had come to pass and her father was still alive.

Delia's thoughts, so sluggish only an instant ago, began to race. The helicopter crash that had supposedly taken her father's life had been a devastating one. The chopper had plowed into the side of a mountain and exploded during a snowstorm. By the time the rescue party got to the wreckage, there were few remains left to investigate. The police said there were two bodies, one of a man and the other of a woman, but Delia had never seen either of them. Some identifiable personal effects had been recovered, but the bodies were too completely destroyed to leave even dental evidence of identity behind. Delia had assumed, along with everybody else, that the two people who died in the crash were her father and stepmother. Could that assumption have been wrong?

Delia believed what the police had said about nobody being able to survive such a devastating crash. But what if her father hadn't been on that helicopter in the first place? What if somebody else had been with Cassandra? But why would that be the case, and why wouldn't he have gotten in touch with somebody since then? Especially, why hadn't he been in touch with her? They were so close. Delia pressed the Christmas card to her breast and held it there while tears formed in her eyes. She'd missed her father terribly in the years between his death and her escape from Colorado. She'd tried not to think about him after that, but he came into her mind anyway, particularly at this time of year. He'd loved the holiday season. He was the one who'd taught her to love it, as well.

Delia began walking slowly toward the elevator, her feet placing themselves automatically one in front of the other without her being aware of the movement. What if, by some miracle, her father hadn't been on that helicopter? What if he'd survived and gone into hiding for some reason? What if he had finally not been able to resist getting in touch with her any longer? It would be just like him to do so with a Christmas card. Maybe he knew something about whoever was trying to get to her now, and he wanted to warn her. But where was he? Delia stopped just short of the elevator bank and looked down at the envelope she was still holding. There was no return address, and in her haste to get at the card she had torn through the corner where the postmark would be. She pieced the ragged edges together again.

There was no postmark. She squinted at the envelope to make sure that was true. The corner was blank and empty—no postmark, no stamp. That meant the card might have been hand delivered to the mail service office. She could go back and ask if they remembered who'd brought it. Delia understood how unlikely that was at this hectic time of the year when deliveries of packages and cards and letters were arriving one after another, but she could ask all the same. Delia examined the rest of the envelope—front, back, inside—but found no further clues to its origin. She looked at the card again, read the printed greeting carefully through but found no clues there, either, only the standard good wishes. She turned the card over and stopped dead still again. There was more handwriting on the back, in the same scrawl as inside.

"Come to South Street Seaport tonight," the scrawl instructed. "I will meet you at the end of Pearl Street under the FDR Drive at 8:00 p.m."

Delia read the message through several times. She probably should have gone back to the mail service office then and asked if anybody remembered this card, but she was sure they wouldn't. Besides, the part of her most closely governed by her heart wanted to believe the card came from her father and that he'd be waiting for her tonight by the East River as it said. She might have been afraid the mail service people would tell her otherwise. Whatever the reason, she didn't turn around and retrace her steps down the eleventh floor hallway. She hurried forward to the elevators instead, already calculating how she would give Nick the slip so she could go to the Seaport on her own. Maybe that wasn't a wise or sensible thing to do, but she wasn't thinking wisely right now. She was thinking as Topsy, and Topsy was only a child—a child with a very special and private relationship with her father, too private a relationship to share, even with Nick.

Chapter Thirteen

The snow had begun at around noon, while they were still at the Waldorf—large, fluffy clumps of flakes tumbling lazily down. By the time Delia exited the Lincoln Building, that picturesque snowfall was blowing itself into a blizzard. She stepped back into the shelter of the entrance long enough to pull her watch cap from her pocket. She shoved the hat down onto her head and poked her hair up underneath it. She kept hold of the precious card all the time she was doing that, even though having something else in her hand made the process of covering her head much more difficult. It occurred to her then that the snow might smear the handwritten message, which was even more precious to her than the card. Reluctantly, she opened her coat and slid the card carefully into the inside pocket. One of the reasons she wore a man's style overcoat like this one was because of that special inside pocket for stashing things away. She ducked her head as she emerged from the doorway onto Madison Avenue. The wind hit her with a barrage of icy snow that stung her cheeks like flying needles. She tucked her chin into her neck and pulled up her collar as she hurried toward Forty-first Street where Nick was waiting with the cab.

At least, he was supposed to be waiting there. Delia rounded the corner to find the cab gone and Nick with it. She tried not to be too obvious about scanning the street. By now, she'd forced herself back to her usual sensible self, attentive once again to remaining inconspicuous. Granted, it was hard to believe anybody would be lurking at ambush for her in weather like this, but sore experience had taught her she was wise to be cautious in all circumstances—even a storm packing what felt like gale force winds. If not for those precautions, she would have begun to shout Nick's name right here and now.

They'd left the Waldorf at going on three o'clock. She told Nick that her traveler's club gave her late checkout privileges. Actually, while he was in the bathroom, she'd called the desk and paid for the extra time. It was after three now, but the heavy snow and hovering clouds had turned the sky dark as dusk. Still, it was too early for the street lamps to be on, which added to the gloom. Delia gave the street one more sweeping glance. She couldn't hang around here much longer. She was too easy a target standing in one place like this. Besides, if she stayed here on this corner she was bound to be buried beneath a snowdrift before long.

What could have happened to Nick? Maybe they hadn't evaded notice leaving the Waldorf after all. Maybe whoever attacked her in the stairway last night was after them again today. He could have crept up on Nick as he waited in the cab. Fearful images darted one after the other through Delia's thoughts. The last thing she wanted in all the world was for Nick to be hurt, especially on her account. Until that moment, she hadn't considered the danger he could be in because he was protecting her. Before last night and their lovemaking, he'd been the bodyguard and she'd been the client. Exposing himself to danger on her behalf was his job. Now all of that had changed, and she could only think of how much she wanted him to be safe. That was why, when she heard his voice behind her, she spun around and all but jumped into his arms.

"Delia" was what he'd said before she made that impulsive leap.

NICK HAD WAITED in the cab as long as he could. He'd have preferred to be with Delia, but she'd insisted on going into the Lincoln Building alone. What could be so damned private about a stop at her answering service anyway? He understood that she'd spent years being secretive. Keeping herself and the details of her life under wraps was second nature to her by now. Still, her suspiciousness, however ingrained it might be, wasn't making his job any easier.

On the other hand, maybe a few minutes on his own wasn't a bad idea. After all, he'd had the second biggest shock of his life only a couple of hours ago. The first biggest was five years past and delivered by the same woman. Nick looked out the cab window at the fast-swirling snow. Weather like this reminded him of Colorado. Before today, he'd have stopped himself from making that connection. Suddenly, Colorado, the Lesters and Rebecca were no longer off limits to his memory. That was something of a shock in itself.

Pieces had been popping into place in his head ever since Delia told him who she really was—like why PEI had never hired him to do a job for them before. She couldn't take the chance he'd recognize her. Nick was amazed by how much she had changed. He was essentially the same guy he'd always been. Meanwhile, Rebecca had made herself into almost a whole new woman. He figured women in general were better at that kind of thing than men. Still, he found it pretty amazing. His mind was lost in that wonder, swirling like the snowfall, when the cabdriver's voice interrupted the reverie.

"Hey, buddy. I can't sit here no longer. I got a cop on my tail."

Sure enough. Nick looked out the window to find a blue and white police car with the officer in the window motioning for the cabbie to move on.

"Maybe they wanna bring a snowplow through," said the cabdriver. "So, if your lady ain't comin' down the street right this minute, I gotta take off. You can come with me and we'll circle the block, but I can't guarantee how long that'll take."

Nick had rolled down the street-side window. The snow blew so hard into his face that he'd had to squint to see. He'd strained to make out the figures coming around the corner from Madison Avenue. Delia wasn't among them.

"That's okay," he said, counting out money for the fare. "I'll get out and wait here."

"Sorry, buddy," the driver said as Nick handed over the bills. "I hate to leave ya out in the cold like this, but when the boys in blue give a guy the word, he's smart to take it."

"No problem," Nick said, climbing out of the cab. He hoped he was right about that as he trudged through the snow to the curb, all the time watching for Delia to return.

The wind was sharp and frigid. Nick shoved his hands deep into his pockets. His fingers folded around the grip of the Beretta he'd stuck in his right pocket for fast accessibility. His own gun was still in the back of his waistband as usual. He was glad he had on gloves. The cold steel of the Beretta wouldn't feel very good to the touch right now.

Somebody was coming around the corner from Madison Avenue, hunched over against the snow and wind. Nick strained to make out the figure, then shrugged so hard that snow shook off his arms. It wasn't Delia, just a man in a cap and a long coat, not the right size to be the guy from the Waldorf, either. Nick looked back toward the corner again.

He'd moved into the shadow of the doorway so he wouldn't be conspicuous from the street. His wristwatch read almost 4:00 p.m., but the sky was already dark as evening from the storm. Darkness came early at this time of year, anyway. The guy in the wool cap and long coat had come up even with Nick's hideaway in the shadows. The guy stopped and looked around. Even through the blizzard and gloom, Nick recognized the profile that was becoming more and more dear to his heart.

"Delia," he called out.

In an instant she was in his arms and he was whispering words that were stolen by the wind almost before they could be spoken.

"LET'S GO to my hotel," Nick said. "We can hole up there while we figure out what to do next."

"All right."

Delia knew she had to find some way to get away from him before she went to the Seaport. At least his hotel was closer to that destination than where they were now. Unfortunately, there were no free cabs to be found, either around the Lincoln Building or down Forty-first or Forty-second streets.

"Nick, why don't we take the subway?" They'd walked all the way to Lexington Avenue by then. "That would be much faster. See what I mean?" She pointed to the snarl of aboveground traffic.

The sidewalks were overflowing with people leaving work early because of the storm. They swarmed toward Grand Central Station, many of them huddled beneath umbrellas distorted into ungainly shapes by the wind. Delia and Nick had to be careful where they walked to keep from being mowed down.

"A cab is safer," he shouted against the wind before running out into the street for the half-dozenth time in a vain attempt to flag down a taxi.

Delia grabbed his arm and tugged him toward the crosswalk at Lexington Avenue.

"I'll get the next one that comes along," he protested.

Delia paid no attention and tugged on. Finally he relented and followed her, probably because they were attracting attention, with her out in front laboring to pull him across the street like a reindeer hauling Santa's sleigh. She kept her grip on his arm and hurried toward the side entrance to Grand Central. Otherwise they might have been separated by the relentless advance of the crowd. She could see Nick glancing furtively this way and that, no doubt on the lookout for the man who was after her. She thought about telling Nick that long experience with making herself anonymous in this city had taught her well the art of getting lost in the crowd.

"I don't like this at all," Nick said while keeping up his frenzied surveillance.

Delia didn't answer. She conceded only to the rapid
pace he insisted upon, until speedy progress proved impossible along the congested underground walkway to
the downtown platform for the R-line train. They simply had to let themselves be carried along by the mo-
mentum of the mass and concentrate on keeping hold
of each other as they went. Delia remembered being
panicked by situations like this when she'd first come to
New York City. Ordinarily, she still didn't care for the
feeling of being controlled by the movements of the
crowd. Right now, however, with Nick's arm linked
firmly through hers, Delia was at ease with letting herself be swept along.

Part of that ease could be credited to the fact that
she'd figured out what she was going to do to get away
from him later on and keep her appointment on the
waterfront. The timing of that plan was one reason
she'd insisted they take the subway. Usually, the trip on
the R-train from Grand Central to Prince Street in Soho
would take twenty minutes tops. Unfortunately that
timetable didn't take into account an extra-hectic rush
hour and waiting for a second train because the first was
too jammed to force their way into. Delia could tell how
crazy this situation was making Nick. He might as well
have had his head on a swivel the way he was trying to
keep watch in every direction at once. As for attracting
attention, under any other circumstances, his behavior
would definitely have made them the object of considerable curiosity. But this was Manhattan at rush hour
in the middle of a blizzard. Everybody around them was
intent upon getting home, and vigilance was required
for them to accomplish that under these conditions.
Nick would have to do something a lot more bizarre
than swivel his head around to attract much notice here.

Delia wasn't really concerned about that anyway. She had her plan and her timetable to make her more worried by the minute. When they finally made it to Prince Street and piled out of the train and up the stairs to street level, her watch told her it was past five o'clock.

"We'll stop at the deli for sandwiches," Nick said.

Delia had to bite her lip to keep from crying out in protest. They hadn't eaten since their room service breakfast at the Waldorf late that morning. She had to concede that Nick might be hungry again by now.

"Okay," she said.

"We'll order them to go."

Delia nodded. At least, that was a relief. On the other hand, the line at the deli counter was long. Working Manhattanites might just be the world's leading devourers of takeout cuisine. On a night like this, when the effort simply to make it home used up even more stamina than usual, lots of New Yorkers had little desire to cook supper. Delia understood that reality, but understanding didn't make her patient. She was about ready to fidget out of her skin by the time they finally got their sandwich order filled and had pushed through the crowd out of the shop.

They made their way along narrow streets that were almost as congested as the deli had been. Sometimes traversing this city was more hassle than just about anyone could bear. This was one of those times for Delia. Meanwhile, Nick kept up his head-swiveling routine all the way—out of the train, at the deli, along the street. Delia didn't bother to tell him how futile she believed that exercise to be. She definitely didn't mention how far her current concentration on her own particular quest had carried her from sharing Nick's obsession with her safety. She was going to meet the person who sent her the Christmas card invitation, no matter how much danger that journey might place her in, and she had to get there on time.

Delia was very relieved to find that Nick's hotel was only a block and a half from the subway stop and even closer to the deli. The Hotel Tivoli might not be in the same league as the Waldorf in the estimation of travel guide writers, but Delia was as happy to arrive there as if it had been the Taj Mahal. On any other occasion, she would have paused to take in the small, quaint lobby with its warm touches of old, deep-grained mahogany and cozily worn Oriental carpet. Tonight, however, she had an agenda to keep moving. She didn't even take time to register the way her obvious hurrying of Nick toward the elevator brought a quizzical expression to the desk clerk's face.

"I'm really hungry," Delia had said as her excuse for rushing Nick along.

Of course, that meant she actually had to eat some of the very thick ham and Swiss on rye, which had been her order at the deli. The sandwich was delicious and made her wish she had time to savor it. She also couldn't help thinking about how much she would enjoy taking full advantage of yet again being in a hotel room alone with Nick. She caught him gazing at her, between bites of his corned beef, with a look in his eyes that told her he might be pondering that same advantage. This was the signal for her to press forward with her plan. She'd already rehearsed what she was going to say a dozen times in her head.

"Nick, I'm afraid I have a very big favor to ask of you," she began.

"What's that?" he asked, wiping his mouth with one of the coarse paper napkins from the deli.

"I left something at my apartment, something I can't get along without." She rushed on before she could lose her nerve. She'd told many untruths since going into hiding. It was much more difficult to lie to him now, especially since just this morning she'd pledged to be truthful with him from now on. "I take medication," she said. "For my stomach."

"I didn't know that." He looked skeptical.

"I don't like to talk about it," she said, "but if I don't get my pills I'll be very sick. I'd go get them myself, but—"

"No," he interrupted, raising his hand as if to stop her. "I'll go. You stay here and rest."

"I'd actually like to take a bath," she said, not proud of herself for how good she was at making her story even more believable.

Still, she had to let him finish his sandwich. She was subjected to further maddening moments while he bundled himself into an extra sweater and wound a long scarf around his neck in preparation for reentering the blizzard that continued to rage outside. Nick was on his way out the door at last when he turned toward her.

"Don't let anybody in," he said. "Absolutely nobody till I get back. Will you promise me that?"

"I promise," she said, feeling yet another lie stick in her throat.

He pulled a gun from his pocket and pressed it into her hand. She opened her mouth to protest, then shut it again. As much as she hated guns, she'd be wise to go armed on the trip she had in store for herself tonight.

Chapter Fourteen

Nick was gone at last. Delia could hardly believe she'd
finally gotten him out the door. Now she missed him.
The hotel room, though fairly small, felt empty and
echoing. She bundled herself up quickly—extra socks,
a second sweater, her heavy boots—and left only ten
minutes or so behind Nick, but not by the front entrance. He might have asked the desk clerk to watch out
for her. Nick was definitely protective enough to do
that. Delia wondered if he would hover over her quite
so closely if it wasn't his job to do so.

Ordinarily, she might have found such attentiveness
suffocating. Yet Nick's attentions made her feel warm
and peaceful, as if she'd been tucked up inside a thick,
soft blanket that kept her from bumping against the
hard edges and sharp corners of life. She'd had enough
experience with such collisions to make a little swad-
dling very welcome. Unfortunately, for the moment
she'd chosen to slip out from beneath the blanket of
Nick's protection. She was on her own.

Delia crept down the narrow back stairs of the small
hotel and let herself out through the heavy, steel fire
door that clamped shut fast and locked tight with a click
behind her. The alleyway was dimly lit and cold, with

snow sifting down from the strip of open sky between the buildings several stories above her head. Covered trash cans lined the scarred brick walls and were already crowned by inches of white. A single bulb in a metal cage over the doorway did little to disperse the gloom. Delia shivered, though the layers of clothing she was wearing didn't really let in much cold. She hastened down the alleyway, relieved that there were no tracks other than her own in the snow. She couldn't imagine even the most enterprising street criminals out plying their nefarious trade on a night like this, but there was no such thing as being too cautious in New York City.

The thought reminded her that she was embarking upon a mission that was anything but cautious. A woman alone traipsing around the waterfront after dark could be a target for all kinds of danger no matter what the weather. She pulled her cap down around her face. Any signs of her femaleness were muffled under the bulk of sweaters and her long, shapeless coat. The cap plus a scarf wrapped around the lower half of her face completed the camouflage. Luckily, when she left the alley for the thoroughfare, nobody was paying much attention to her anyway as they trudged along through the storm.

Delia turned her thoughts and planning toward what came next—how she would get from here to the Seaport. Most seasoned New Yorkers were in the habit of mapping out their mode of transportation before going anywhere. They would weigh one alternative against the other—taxi, car service, bus, subway. The decision often depended on the destination and the relative safety and speed of the route traveled to get there. Tonight, Delia's decision would be determined by the elements. A taxi would be impossible to find. Car service would take too long getting here. Besides, street level traffic had to be in a state of nearly terminal gridlock as the snow piled up and the roadbed became more and more slippery. There was a bus straight down Broadway to Lower Manhattan but no bus lane to facilitate progress through the snarl of vehicles. She was too far away to walk it, either. Subway was the inevitable solution.

Delia slogged toward the corner. She'd have to consult the map below ground on the wall next to the token booth. She didn't travel this way often enough to have memorized the train routes. She knew buses better because they were her preferred form of public transport. Her years of paranoia made her feel safer in a vehicle where she could see out the windows into the surrounding world. She also liked the fact that, unlike on a subway, she could jump off a bus at any corner. Still, the underground had to be her choice tonight. She shivered again at the thought of how unfamiliar she was with her destination. She knew very well that the surest way to get yourself into trouble in the city was to stop using your head. Going into strange territory after dark was definitely not a wise move. For Delia, however, this evening's journey was not about using her head as much as it was about following her heart. She hunched her face into the folds of her scarf and hurried toward the subway entrance.

NICK DIDN'T LIKE leaving Delia alone, but he could tell she was trying to get rid of him. He guessed she needed some time on her own. He could understand why she might want to slow her world down for a while right about now. He would have preferred to hold her in his arms as she slept or, better yet, to take that bath she'd mentioned with her. The thought of water glistening across the perfect roundness of Delia's breasts and her sleek thigh lifting out of a foam of bath bubbles made him all but groan right here in the hallway outside her apartment door. He'd have run out into the stormy night and searched the city up and down for bubble bath if that would make this fantasy come true.

Nick cleared his throat and adjusted his jeans to accommodate the sudden snugness in the area of his zipper. He couldn't escape the fantasies of her that flitted regularly across his mind. She was even more beautiful than five years ago, when she'd been on the skinny side, lovely but spare in the flesh department. She'd acquired just enough of that flesh since then. She was a provocative and appealing girl five years ago. Last night, when he slipped her nightgown from her shoulders, he'd discovered a voluptuous woman.

He could see her now, and feel her, too, the way she moved in his arms. Her hips rolled in a rhythm so sensuous he'd been lured along as her partner in a dance of love. Everywhere he touched her, she responded like a rapturous instrument beneath his fingers, playing exquisite music just for him. He'd been attracted to her five years ago as Rebecca Lester, though his code of professional ethics had kept him from doing anything about it. He'd wanted her then but with a much paler passion than what had set him burning last night. Delia was fully a woman now. She knew what a man needed and also what she needed herself. Yet he sensed she hadn't learned these things in the arms of other men. He sensed she'd been very alone for a very long time. The intensity of her hunger told him that. He wished he could be satisfying that hunger for both of them right now.

Nick did groan this time. If he didn't stop tormenting himself with such thoughts, he'd be running back to the Tivoli before he had a chance to accomplish what he'd come here to do. He reminded himself of how much Delia said she needed those pills from her medicine cabinet and did his best to return his attention to her apartment door. The slip of paper was still there, exactly where he'd left it. That meant no one had been here. Nobody had pulled on the door, anyway.

Nick let himself in using the key Delia had given him and was immediately assailed by the scent of evergreen. He experienced a small twinge in the area of his heart. He might have switched on the lights for a better view of the blue spruce, but he'd already decided to maintain a low profile while he was here. A flashlight would be the best way to do that. He had to content himself with a glance at the tall, tapering silhouette against the glimmer of streetlight filtering past the window blinds. Even that brief glimpse made him think of colored lights reflecting in the windowpane—colored lights dancing over Delia's soft skin.... Nick shook himself hard enough to make those lights wink off in his imagination. He flicked on the flashlight in his hand instead and trained the beam onto the floor and away from the windows as he headed for the bathroom. He resolved to wrap a tighter rein around his fantasies, but he doubted even *his* willpower was that strong.

A few minutes later he was letting himself out of Delia's apartment with her pill bottles tucked into his jacket pocket. His mind was still on those fantasies he'd been having only moments before. He was pondering what their power might be indicating about his feelings for Delia and what he should do in response to those feelings. Usually, Nick didn't do a lot of pondering. He was more of a straightforward, action kind of guy. These uncharacteristic, deeper thoughts took up most of his attention as he bent to secure yet another small strip of paper between the lower section of the door frame and the door. All he felt was the first edge of the blow. Then everything went black.

DELIA WAS RUNNING late for her rendezvous on the waterfront. Unfortunately, actually running was out of the question. Otherwise she'd have been racing down John Street as fast as her feet could carry her. Even on an ordinary night, this part of Lower Manhattan was all but deserted after workday hours. Tonight, the falling snow added to the emptiness. The buildings here were tall with gray stone facades, and the street was narrow. The streetlights were on, but mostly they illuminated the halo of blowing snow immediately circling each lamp. The rest of the street was as gray as the fronts of the buildings. All sound was muffled, including the whistle of the wind up from the riverfront a few blocks ahead. Delia could feel that wind, even if she couldn't hear it, slapping against the narrow strip of her face that remained exposed. She pulled her scarf up higher till only her eyes were visible and did her best to hurry on.

She thought she'd become accustomed to isolation in these five, solitary years, but that was nothing compared with how alone she felt right now. She might have been a space explorer stranded on some bleak, white moonscape with gray phantom shapes rising on either side. She considered backtracking to Fulton Street, which might be less deserted, but she was already past the hour when she was supposed to meet whoever had written her that card. She couldn't allow herself to think of that person as her father, though her heart ached to do so. She wanted more than anything for her father to be alive. She'd forced herself to shut out the thought of him all these years. Now it came rushing back, springing tears to her eyes. She dabbed at them with her gloved hands, afraid they might freeze. That would be all she needed tonight, to have her eyes suddenly iced shut in addition to the rest of what she had to deal with. The absurdity of that image threatened to drive a burst of hysterical laughter from her throat. She gulped to keep it there and slogged on.

The snow was deepening and drifted. No shoveling had been done yet. Offices in the vicinity had probably let their workers go home early. The walkways would have been less buried then, no need to shovel till the snow stopped or at least till very early the next morning, before everything opened up again. Delia pressed on, her body bent against the chill of the wind, lifting her feet with each difficult step as if she were walking through a knee-high desert of snow. Actually, she was doing exactly that. Another image to add to the general creepiness of this experience. Thank heaven, she could finally see the comparative breadth and brightness of Pearl Street just ahead. She hurried toward it, like a bedouin toward an oasis.

Delia had visited South Street Seaport several times in her solitary explorations of the city. On a normal evening this area east of the cobbled gateway at the junction of Pearl and Fulton streets would have been an exception to the general desertion of nighttime Lower Manhattan. The street would be occupied by diners from the restaurants, revelers from the taverns and cocktail lounges, strollers browsing the shops and gazing up at the spotlit masts of the Seaport Museum's antique sailing ships moored along its piers. Christmas was an especially festive time in this part of town. Carollers costumed in memory of the nineteenth century Age of Sail performed on street corners. Father Christmas might even appear among them or the Ghost of Christmas Past. The shops were done up at their yuletide best. Brightly lit Christmas trees perched high up in the crow's nests of the museum ships. Delia had come down here last year at this time and found it all delightful.

There were no carollers tonight, no revelers or strollers or browsers, no Father Christmas, either, though she could readily imagine a ghost of some kind or other materializing out of the gloom. Still, there were more lights here and the thoroughfare was wide, closed to traffic had there been any. Along this broad, open stretch, the snow had drifted away from the center of the street and up against the buildings on either side. Delia found that more shallow center track and was able to pick up her pace some. She had no competition for her position on the pathway. The shops were all closed, and the restaurant windows were empty. Not even a stray, stalwart tourist was out here to brave the wrath of winter. Delia couldn't help suspecting more strongly than ever that she was on a fool's errand.

She glanced up for reassurance toward the rigging of the *Peking*, the crown jewel of the Seaport's permanently docked sailing fleet. If the lit-up trees were there, their sparkle was lost behind the blizzard, which roiled even more thickly here at the edge of the East River where it began to widen into New York Harbor and the Atlantic Ocean beyond. Delia sighed. She could have used that glimmer of holiday cheer right now as her

heart threatened to waver from its determination to
follow the instructions on the Christmas card crumpled into the inside pocket of her coat. She'd turned left
from Fulton onto South Street, and there was still no
one in sight, nobody up the block to Beekman or past
it, nobody under the FDR Drive, which vaulted on its
massive steel framework high above South Street. Delia
could see well enough even in this dimmed light to know
that she was alone here.

She might have pulled out the card and read it again,
but that wasn't necessary. She'd committed its message
to memory. She was in the right place, but she wasn't
here at the right time. Or maybe the sender of the card
had been put off by the weather, or thought Delia would
be, and decided not to come. Whatever the reason, Delia appeared to have made this trek for nothing. Under
other circumstances, she might have stopped to note
that she'd meanwhile had the unique experience of
snowbound Lower Manhattan and that what lay around
her right now really was a beautiful sight. Unfortunately, she wasn't in the proper frame of mind to be re-
ceptive to that beauty at the moment. She was mostly
frustrated and suddenly aware, with a growing acute-
ness, of how cold she was becoming.

"Damn," she muttered, and stamped her foot, both
to punctuate that frustration and against the numbness
creeping upward from her toes.

All of a sudden she remembered Nick. She was almost shocked to realize that she actually had not
thought of him more than a few times since she'd left
the Tivoli and not at all since exiting the subway at the
World Trade Center. Up to that point he'd been solidly
planted in her thoughts for what felt like an extremely
long time. Her fixation on her waterfront destination

and quest had driven even handsome, fascinating, maddeningly compelling Nick Avery from her near-obsessed mind. He was very likely back at the Tivoli by now, or certainly close to arriving there. He'd be terribly worried to find her gone.

Delia peered through the snow searching for a pay phone and spotted one near the corner of Beekman Street. She hurried toward it, pulling off a glove to rummage in her coat pocket for a quarter. She was in the habit of keeping phone change there along with a spare subway token or two. Her fingers had numbed considerably. They weren't as adept as usual at telling the shape and size of one kind of coin from the other. It took her the full distance to the phone to fish out the quarter she needed. She was intent upon not allowing her cold, clumsy fingers to drop it when she spotted a stooped figure emerging from the gloom across South Street under the FDR Drive. Whoever it was hesitated, still too far away and obscured by the veil of falling snow for Delia to make out anything other than that this person wasn't very tall. Her father hadn't been very tall, either.

Delia's heart skipped into her throat. "Daddy," she cried out. "It's me. Topsy. I'm here."

The figure didn't move. Delia was still holding the quarter in one hand and the receiver in the other. She dropped the coin and plopped the receiver back into its carriage on the front of the phone box. The face of that box was covered in shiny chrome almost as reflective as a mirror even in this subdued light. In that instant, Delia registered movement reflected across the chrome face. Yet, she was standing still. Her long-honed, self-protective instincts leapt instantly into place, and she spun around fast to catch the man behind her just enough off guard that he stepped backward in surprise.

Delia had the impression that this was the man from the Waldorf stairway nearly hidden now beneath almost as much clothing as she was wearing. She didn't take time or brain power to do more than let that impression flit rapidly past. She remembered the gun in her pocket. Her hand was into her coat and out again, brandishing the pistol before even she knew she was going to make that move.

"Get away from me or I'll shoot you dead right here," she screamed with a vehemence she also hadn't anticipated.

He hesitated only a second, then turned and ran back up Beekman Street into the camouflage of the storm and was gone. Delia knew that she could have held him here at gunpoint while she used the phone to call Nick. She also knew how long it would take him to get down here and how difficult it would be to keep this man at bay till then. She couldn't call the police, of course. Her fear of being arrested herself precluded seeking official help. She'd computed all of that in the seconds it took to draw the gun and shout her warning. She let her would-be assailant escape and watched him go. By the time she turned back toward South Street, the small, stooped figure was gone, too.

Then, something very strange happened. Like a film rolling backward, Delia found herself seeing again what had happened just before she'd registered movement in the chrome faceplate of the telephone. In that moment the figure across South Street had started suddenly forward with one arm raised and head lifted. Maybe this person was trying to warn Delia against the danger behind her. She suspected this might be so, but that wasn't what made her gasp as the scene flashed back to her now. In that fleeting instant she'd seen the face of the person scrambling toward her across South Street. She'd seen the face, and she knew who it was.

Chapter Fifteen

Nick heard the the sirens before he actually knew what they were. The sound jangled through his brain, but it was only noise to him at first, and far off, too. Noise and identification hadn't yet come together. His head hurt, and that caught his immediate attention. He'd been hit. Maybe he couldn't connect things up because he had amnesia or brain damage. It occurred to him, first through a fog and then more sharply, that if he could make this observation about amnesia or brain damage, he probably didn't have either. At that instant he also knew that the noise was a police siren, and he could guess the most likely reason he was hearing it. Somebody in this building must have seen or heard what happened to Nick, maybe the thud of him falling to the floor after being zapped from behind. Maybe he'd cried out. He couldn't remember. Very possibly, the witness hadn't even opened his or her apartment door to look out. They just called 9-1-1 right off. New Yorkers were like that. They'd be cautious about putting themselves in danger while trying to help all the same.

The cops were just about here, and Nick had to disappear fast. Part of him might have opted for some official help with whatever was happening to Delia, but asking for that help wasn't in the job description, especially not now that he knew who Delia really was. She'd still be among the FBI Wanteds for the Denver case. There's no statute of limitations on murder. Nick shrugged off the thought, shook his head clear and pulled himself the rest of the way up off the floor. He wasn't yet feeling a hundred percent, but he had to make tracks out of here, anyway.

He took longer getting back downtown than he had coming up. After slipping down the rear stairs and out of the fire door at Delia's building, he employed a standard diversionary tactic—ducking into a building, watching to see if he was being followed, then ducking out another entrance. Ordinarily he'd have taken several cabs in winding directions, but the snow had slowed traffic too much to make that workable. Whoever clouted Nick from behind would have too little trouble tailing him from one traffic jam to the next. He traveled much of the way on foot before darting into a subway for the remainder of his trip to the Prince Street stop.

Having Delia out of sight worried him much more than the lump forming behind his left ear, more even than finding out who'd given him that lump. It was bad business for a bodyguard to leave his client untended. He was feeling very uneasy about having done that even before the desk clerk at the Tivoli called out as Nick hurried past.

"I don't think your friend is upstairs," she said.

There was a hint of indignation in the way she said that. Her name was Mindy. She'd let Nick know on several occasions, in both subtle and not so subtle ways, that she found him interesting. He'd only noticed that because she had a punky look about her that reminded him a little of Rebecca, the way she'd been five years ago. Tonight he barely noticed Mindy or her petulant manner at all. He had Rebecca, in the flesh as Delia, to concern himself with now.

"You said to keep an eye out for her. Right?"

"Yes, that's right."

Nick had mentioned his concern for Delia on the way out earlier. Mindy's resentful tone suggested maybe that hadn't been too smart a move on his part.

"I live to please," she gibed, "so I called your room a while ago and guess what?"

"What?" Nick couldn't help his impatience.

"Well." She dragged out the word and dangled the pencil she was holding from her fingers. "You're not going to like it."

And you're not going to like the way I jump over that desk and throttle you if you don't get to the point, Nick almost said out loud.

"Come on, Mindy. What gives?" he managed instead. "You wouldn't want to get me in trouble with my client, would you?"

"Is that what she is? Your client?"

"Yes. She's my client." Nick had pulled his gloves off on his way into the lobby. He clenched his fists and dug his fingernails into his palms now to keep himself from doing that jumping and throttling he'd been thinking about a moment ago. Cajoling rather than bullying was the way to go here, no matter how maddening it might be.

"Then you just may be in trouble after all," Mindy said, "because she took off."

That was exactly what Nick didn't want to hear. "Did you see her leave? Which way did she go?"

"I didn't see a thing. All I know is nobody answered when I rang your room, and I rang two or three times."

Nick barely remembered to mutter, "Thanks," as he bolted for the stairway, which was a faster route than waiting for the Tivoli's antiquated elevator. There was still hope that Mindy could be wrong. Delia might have slept through the phone ringing or maybe she was still in the bathtub at the time. Unfortunately, the race of his pulse and the dryness in his throat were telling Nick that neither of those was the case. Sure enough, when he got to his room, nobody was there.

His first thought was that something could have gone wrong at PEI. The way Delia was so dedicated to that job of hers she'd have gone running back there to take care of things despite the weather or the danger. He grabbed the phone, pressed nine for an outside line and punched in the PEI number. He clutched the receiver altogether too hard through three long rings till the connection was made. His heart leapt when he heard, "Hello." It was Delia's voice.

"Delia?"

"You have reached the office of Protective Enterprises Incorporated," her voice said.

"Damn it."

Nick pounded his thigh once, hard, with his balled-up fist, as the voice on the telephone droned on. He'd reached the PEI answering machine. He'd hoped against hope that at least Lily, the temporary worker, would be there, but of course she would have closed up and gone home by now, especially with this storm going on. Still, maybe Delia was there in the office and monitoring phone messages. That would explain why she didn't have the service picking up instead of the machine. He snatched at this very slender possibility as if it had some real chance of proving true.

"Delia," he said as soon as the voice message ended and the answer recording began. "Are you there? It's Nick. Pick up if you're there."

He listened desperately for her to do what he asked but heard only silence in return.

"Delia, are you there?" he asked again while his pleading tone was recorded for posterity.

Still no answer came until finally the connection clicked off and a second later the dial tone began. Nick slammed the phone down. Where the hell was she? He paced the short distance from phone table to window. Outside, snow swirled and blew in the dim remnants of illumination that made their way up through the storm from the streetlights below. She was out in this, but he had no idea where. He also had no idea why, and that was driving him craziest of all. He'd told her to stay put. Why hadn't she done that? What could be important enough to take her out of this room into danger?

Another possibility crossed his mind and made his heart pound faster than ever. What if she'd been taken out of here by somebody else? He measured the likelihood of that. There were two ways into the Tivoli at ground level. The rear entrance was guarded by a heavy, metal, safety-locked door. Nobody could come through that without a tank or at least an automatic weapon and a lot of noise. The only other entry was straight into the lobby, and Mindy wouldn't have missed that. She didn't miss much. She also wouldn't let anybody past her she didn't know. She might be resentful of Nick having a woman in his room, but Mindy would do her job all the same.

What about the fire escape? There was one from the street to Nick's window, just like every room in the hotel. Fire regulations said it had to be that way. Nick remembered the handprint on the greasy surface of Delia's bedroom windowsill. He leaned closer to his window and peered out at the sill. No marks there, and none on the fire escape platform, either. No handprints on the sill, no footprints on the fire escape. The snow was coming down hard and could have covered prints over. Still, Nick reasoned, there would have been at least indentations or some sign left behind, wet marks on the carpet inside the room or something like that. He made a quick inspection but found nothing. He was almost certain nobody had come in this way.

All that remained was the outside chance someone could have slipped by Mindy downstairs. No matter how unlikely Nick figured that to be, he had to check it out for sure. He could have called down to the front desk, but he tore out of his room and headed for the stairway instead. He had to do something that required movement. If he was forced to stand passively on the end of a telephone line one more time, he just might jump straight out of his skin. He was that agitated, and a good deal of that agitation was because he knew he'd fallen down on the job. He'd left Delia alone. If he wasn't so hell-bent to get down to the lobby as fast as he could, he might have stopped and kicked himself very hard in the behind.

DELIA ROUNDED the corner onto Mercer Street with her head down. That seemed to be the best way to keep snow crystals from bombarding her face. The snowfall hadn't slowed any in its intensity and now had taken on an icy edge that prickled her cheeks then melted there in a frigid sheen. If she hadn't been hustling along as fast as she could go, she would have been quite cold even in her heavy overcoat, which was now frosted white all over.

Delia trained her eyes just far enough ahead on the sidewalk to keep from running into anybody, though she was pretty much alone on this narrow street. She looked up fully just once to see the entrance to the Tivoli a couple of buildings away, then ducked her face back into her scarf while she scurried even faster and imagined how bright and warm the lobby would be. Consequently, Delia was pretty much barreling along when she plowed straight into somebody moving equally fast out of the hotel entrance. That somebody was Nick.

"Delia, where the hell have you been?" were the first words out of his mouth in almost the same tone of voice she'd heard him use against the creep who'd attacked her on the stairway at the Waldorf. Delia's imaginings of her longed-for arrival at the Tivoli had not included an angry greeting.

"You don't need to shout at me, and you can stop dragging me around, too."

He'd taken her by the arm and was pulling her back into the hotel lobby. The young woman at the reception desk watched them with considerable interest. Fortunately, no one else was present to see the scene Nick was making. Delia shook herself free of his grasp.

"I came back here, and you were gone," he said only a little less loudly and through gritted teeth. "I want to know where you went."

"I had some business to take care of." Shaking herself had dislodged a cloud of snow that settled in a wet ring around her on the lobby floor.

"I don't believe you. I called your office, and you weren't there."

"You don't believe me?" Delia's voice hit a louder register now. Five years of constant attention to keeping a low profile in public flew out the doorway into the snow. "Where do you get the nerve to accuse me of lying?"

She *was* lying of course, but at the moment that seemed beside the point.

"Look, for once I just want the straight truth out of you.

From the sound of that, Nick's anger was losing some of its heat while Delia's did the opposite.

"I told you I had business to attend to. Whether that business was in my office or not is none of your concern."

Her cheeks were flaming and not just from being stung by icy snow. She tore at her scarf to get it away from her face.

"What you do *is* my concern. It's also my job."

She could hear the attempt at reconciliation in his tone, but she wasn't interested in reconciliation at the moment. For days now, she'd been angry at having her life invaded. Nick was catching the brunt of that accumulating rage.

"Your job is to do what I tell you." She didn't care how mean or surly that sounded. "You seem to be forgetting you work for me."

She expected that to get his masculine dander up. Maybe she even wanted it to happen so there'd be a cathartic confrontation and she could vent the entire depth of her frustration right here in this hotel lobby. If that was her intention, Nick wasn't cooperating. Instead of blasting back at her, he shrugged his broad shoulders then reached his arms around her and pulled her close to his chest. He didn't seem to notice how she was dampening his clothing with melting snow.

"I'm not forgetting anything about you. I haven't been able to forget anything about you for the past five years."

Delia took a long breath as if to inhale those words deep into herself. In that instant, more about her was melting than the snow on their clothing. When she let her breath free again, her angry tension gushed out with it. She sunk against him and might have crumpled to the floor if his strong arms hadn't held her firmly upright. All of a sudden she felt as if she might start crying. She would sob and sob till the bands of loss and fear and regret clamped for five years, maybe more, around her heart finally loosened their hold. She'd be free from sorrow at last, a liberation she hadn't let herself even hope for. She caught her breath in sharply before that sobbing could begin. Otherwise, she feared, the deluge of tears might go on forever.

"Let's go somewhere and talk," Nick whispered softly against her soggy knit cap. Delia felt his head turn in the direction of the reception desk. He must also be aware of the public spectacle they had become. He was probably embarrassed. He did live in this place part of the time, after all, and wouldn't want to make a scene here.

"Okay," she managed to croak as she clung to his closeness just a moment longer.

"There's a café in the next block where we can get something to eat," he said.

His words brought Delia's stomach suddenly back into focus for her, as if it hadn't been part of her anatomy till now. She tried to remember when she'd last eaten. Oh, yes, a couple of bites of a deli sandwich back in Nick's room what felt like a very long time ago.

"Are you hungry?" he asked.

Delia hesitated no more than an instant before pulling away from him far enough to look up into his face.

"Yes, I am," she said, and she wasn't just referring to the gnawing in her stomach. She knew right then that she was hungry for him—his company, his protection and, later on, his body.

"Let's go," he said, taking her arm.

Nick glanced back briefly toward the reception desk, and Delia did the same. The young woman there was scowling at them openly. She looked like she was really upset to have them carrying on so emotionally in her lobby. Delia could understand that. Still, she couldn't help thinking how, at the Waldorf, the staff would act as if they hadn't seen a thing.

"By the way," Nick said as he opened the door to guide Delia through, "I got your pills. Do you need to take one now?"

Delia had to think for a moment what he was talking about. She'd all but forgotten the ruse she'd used for sending him off on his wild-goose chase so she could get away from him on her own.

"No," she said after the details came clear again. "I'm fine."

If Nick was taken aback by how much that differed from her earlier insistence on the urgency of his errand, he didn't let it show. Instead he turned her toward him before they left the shelter of the Tivoli entryway and wound her scarf back around her neck to shield her from the storm.

"Good," he said. "That's what I want—for you to be fine."

The deep timbre of his voice pulsed through her like warm, vibrating sunlight. That sensation remained with her for a long moment. Not till it had worn off did she think to ask if he'd had any trouble finding the pills at her apartment. They were heading down the block by then. As they hurried on, Nick told her what had happened to him. She was still exclaiming with concern when they reached the café. The first thing she did after they'd ducked inside was to pull off first her glove, then the baseball cap he was wearing and start feeling behind his left ear where he said he'd been struck.

Her fingers touched the lump and circled it carefully. She was so intent on checking for any break in the skin or sign of blood and so relieved to find none that she didn't notice right away how tenderly he was smiling down at her. His dark hair was tousled from her pulling his cap off, and a thick lock had fallen across his forehead. Her fingers moved from behind his ear to lift that lock and smooth it gently back into place. He smiled more tenderly still, and she felt herself drifting into the spell of that smile.

"Welcome to Kavehaz," a friendly voice said from just beyond the soft cloud of Delia's reverie. "May I take your things?"

She turned slowly toward the young man in black who stood smiling expectantly next to them. What things could he be talking about, and why would he want to take them? Fortunately, Nick was apparently less entranced than she. He'd already begun unwinding her scarf. Delia came back to her senses enough to help out by removing her other glove, stuffing it into her pocket and unbuttoning her coat. Her cap was the last to come off. She'd had her hair tucked up underneath. It tumbled free now, dampened into wavy strands around her face, oblivious to how hard she'd worked over the years to tame it straight and smooth. Nick was still beaming down at her. He'd taken off his own gloves by now and reached up to touch her cheek.

"You are absolutely beautiful," he said.

Delia forgot all about the waiter then and gazed up into Nick's ruddy, handsome face and glowing eyes.

"So are you," she whispered.

The waiter cleared his throat, but when Delia recalled his presence enough to glance his way he didn't look the least bit impatient. He was still smiling. She glanced around the restaurant, as well. Nobody was watching, and if they had been, Delia suspected they'd be smiling, too. This was Soho, after all, perhaps more amenable than places farther uptown to unorthodox behavior, such as lovers lost in gazing into each other's eyes even before they'd taken off their coats. Delia liked this place already, even before she looked around farther and saw how pleasant it was.

What caught her attention first was the art on the walls, paintings and photographs so well executed and interesting that she was tempted to walk over and look at them more closely. However, Nick had taken her arm and was guiding her along in the waiter's wake. Comfortable-looking couches faced each other across a long coffee table in the front of the room. A young woman with blond, straight hair down her back sat on one of the couches sketching on a large pad, a glass of wine on the coffee table in front of her. Delia was fascinated. She would have liked to peek to see what the artist was working on, but the waiter had already led them beyond the couches to a cozy, marble-topped table near the wall.

After being seated, Delia took a moment to settle into the charm of the place—soft lighting over the bar, another grouping of couches toward the back of the café where several people, all fashionably dressed in low-keyed downtown style, chatted among themselves. White pinlights here and there were a subtle but cheerful reminder of the holiday season. Delia allowed herself to relax for what felt like the first time in almost forever. She almost forgot about being a fugitive from a former life, and about being stalked. She even almost forgot what she'd been so eager to tell Nick before they'd collided in front of the Tivoli.

"Oh, yes," she exclaimed. "You'll never guess what happened."

She was only partly aware of gushing somewhat girlishly or of how incongruous that was with what she had to say. Meanwhile, Nick was still smiling at her across the candlelit table.

"I think I know who put that guy on my tail last night," she continued. "I just saw her down at the Seaport."

Chapter Sixteen

Nick stared at her across the narrow table. He'd put out of his mind for a while how mad she'd made him by slipping off on her own. Now that tight, hot feeling was right under his surface again. He vowed to keep it there.

"The Seaport? Are you talking about South Street Seaport? What were you doing down there on a night like this? The place must have been completely deserted."

"It was. The snow made it look like a white desert on a riverbank."

Nick ignored the poetic description. "Delia, you know better than this. A deserted spot is the most dangerous place of all for you to be."

"I know that, and I'm sorry. I didn't mean to make you worry."

Worry was too small a word for what she'd put him through. And, once again, he found himself doubting her words. She knew exactly how he'd react to knowing she was off somewhere in the night by herself. She knew that would drive him crazy, and he had a hard time believing she hadn't meant it to happen. He wondered, as he had too many times before, just how much truth there was in some of the things she said to him.

"So, what were you doing down there? Thinking about taking a boat tour of the harbor?" He couldn't help the sarcasm.

She looked at him in that studying way she had. She was doing it again, he could tell, deciding how much of the real story she wanted to tell him. He sighed and let his exasperation be tempered by how beautiful she was with her hair a halo of candlelight and her cheeks still rosy from her trek through the snow. She looked up then at the waiter hovering nearby. Nick had been gazing directly into her eyes. He was relieved to have the spell of that gaze broken for a moment. He found it difficult to think sensibly around her too much of the time, and sensible thinking had to be top priority here.

"Let's order," he said, picking up the menu.

Whatever she was or wasn't going to tell him wouldn't change in the few minutes it took to satisfy the waiter and send him on his way. Besides, Nick was hungry. He was a hearty eater most of the time, and meals had been few and far between since he hooked up with Delia. He was surprised at how little that had bothered him. He must have been living on something else besides food. He wasn't yet ready to think about exactly what that something might be.

"The cooking's good here," he said.

She nodded as she read through the menu one item at a time.

"I feel like I'm having my first meal after a long fast, and I have to be very particular about what I choose," she said.

He didn't answer though he felt a little of that himself. He guessed her real priority was to divert his attention from the Seaport question for as long as possible. He ordered fast as a signal he wasn't about to be taken in by that tactic.

"I'll take the grilled chicken," he said.

The waiters here usually spieled off a list of specials at about this time, including just about every ingredient used in preparing each dish. Something in Nick's attitude must have alerted their waiter against doing that, because he simply jotted down Nick's order on a pad then turned toward Delia.

"What's on the pâté plate?" she asked.

Nick sat on his impatience the best he could while the waiter described the mixed salad, special mustard and whatever else came with the damned pâté. Why would she want to eat liver on a night like this, anyway?

"That sounds fine," she said at last. "I'll have the pâté plate."

She handed her menu to the waiter then turned back to Nick. Her smile seemed to brighten the candlelight and almost threw him off course in his determination to get this conversation back on track.

"I wanted to order something I don't often have because this feels like such a special night." Her smile beamed even brighter.

She's good, Nick thought. She has the makings of a first-class con artist.

Of course, that's pretty much what she'd been these past five years. He didn't like to admit to himself what pretending on a full-time basis could have done to her basic sense of honesty. Unfortunately, he had to remain aware of exactly that and not forget it for a minute. Keeping her alive could depend on figuring out the difference between her truths and her not-so-truths. Whatever else about himself might be affected by whether or not he could trust her was yet another area he wasn't ready to get into.

"Do you come here much?" she was asking.

Nick almost didn't answer. He could cut her off instead. The abruptness of his response all but did that.

"Once in a while but not too often," he said. "I go everywhere once in a while but not too often."

"Is that your habit with relationships, too?"

He'd been about to snap her back to her Seaport story, but her question and the sincere way she asked it took him totally by surprise.

"I don't have any relationships," he said before he could think if he really wanted to be that candid, or sound that pathetic, either.

She reached across the table, past the bud vase of fresh flowers and the glassware twinkling with reflections of candle flame. She took his hand, and Nick was lost. His barrier of determination began to dissolve as surely as sugar would dissolve in the Ceylon tea she'd ordered to go with her pâté. She didn't say anything for a while. She just sat there with her hand gently covering his. She wasn't looking at him, only into the candle flame. Finally she spoke in a voice barely loud enough for him to hear.

"I know you want to talk about where I went tonight and why I went there. I'm going to tell you all of that now."

Nick almost turned his hand over to grab hers, but he understood he mustn't disturb the delicacy of this moment. He also understood that she'd made her decision. He could only hope that decision was to trust him. As for himself, her closeness and the touch of her hand was having such a profound effect on him that he had to concentrate on not leaping up from his chair to take her in his arms. His heart was slamming so hard in his chest he wondered if she could hear it.

"I received a message earlier, when I picked up my mail," she began.

Nick forced himself not to jump in with the many questions that came to mind.

"It was an invitation to a meeting tonight at the Seaport. It wasn't signed."

And you went anyway? Nick wanted to shout, but he didn't.

"I know it seems crazy for me to have run off down there by myself on the strength of that alone," she said, as if she might have read his mind. "But the card in my mail referred to me by a nickname only my father used. A private name between just the two of us."

"But your father's dead." The words popped out before Nick could stop them.

"Not for me," she said even more quickly. "In my heart, he's still very much alive. That's what I found out last night when I got the glass angel as a gift. It's so like one he gave me when I was a little girl."

Again, Nick wanted to bolt out of his seat and embrace away the sadness that was so audible even in her very quiet voice.

"Don't be sad for me," she said, once more as if she'd divined his thoughts. "It's a good thing really, in a way. I'd kept myself from thinking about my father for so long that I'd all but lost him. I feel like I've got him back again."

Nick did turn his hand over now. He closed her smaller hand gently into his larger one, and she let him do so. The candlelight glistened in what might have been tears at the corners of her eyes. He wished he didn't have to press her further.

"But it wasn't your father at the Seaport, was it?" he asked as tenderly as he could.

"No, it wasn't."

"Then who was it? You said you recognized somebody there."

Delia sighed and pulled her fingers away from his. All of a sudden, his hand had never felt so empty before.

"There were two people actually," she said, "but I only saw one of them clearly. The first was just a reflection in the front of a telephone. I'm only certain it was a man. Maybe it was the guy from the Waldorf, maybe not. He ran away when he saw the other one coming across the street toward us."

"What other one?"

"The woman."

Nick couldn't help being impatient for the details. What woman? What woman? he wanted to shout. Delia's subdued manner kept him from speaking. She'd been so bright and buoyant when they arrived here. She'd lost that brightness now. Nick wished he could carry her back to those elated moments and rearrange the world so she could stay there. Unfortunately, all he could do was listen and allow her to tell her story at her own pace.

"The woman was Penelope Wren," Delia said next. "Did you know her?"

"From Denver?" Nick searched his memory. The name did sound familiar.

Delia nodded. "She was Tobias Wren's wife."

"I remember now. I dealt with Tobias, but I didn't have much to do with her. That's why I didn't recognize the name right off."

The Wrens had been the caretaker couple at the Lester estate. As Nick recalled, Tobias was in charge of the grounds, and his wife was in charge of the house. They'd taken charge of Rebecca, as well, after her father and stepmother were killed. Edward Lester's will provided for the Wrens to do that.

"Are you sure it was her?" Nick asked.

"Absolutely positive. I saw her face very clearly. She looked exactly the same, and I have my reasons for not forgetting what she looked like."

"What reasons?"

Nick had to wait for his answer till after the waiter, who had just returned, set their plates down in front of them.

"I'll never forget Penelope Wren or mistake somebody else for her," Delia said when they were alone again, "because I've always suspected she and Tobias might have had something to do with framing me for Morty Lancer's murder."

"Are you thinking the Wrens killed him?"

"Not on their own, but they could have been paid by someone else to help out somehow, especially with making it look like I was the killer. The Wrens had copies of all the keys and free access to the house, more so than just about anybody else."

"I see." That sounded a little more possible to Nick. As he remembered it, she was right about that unlimited access. "Didn't they have a kid with medical problems that cost them a lot of money?" He was already thinking in terms of motive.

Delia nodded with renewed vigor. "Exactly. And there's something else I remember, too."

"What's that?"

"Penelope Wren is a small woman with very small hands, just like the ones that left prints on my windowsill."

"You're right. She was very small." Nick knew he had to be careful not to jump to conclusions, but this was the first real lead they'd had.

"Unfortunately, I have no idea how to go about finding her again," Delia said.

"Well, first of all, we can assume she chose the Seaport as a meeting place because she knows the vicinity." This was Nick's area of expertise. Even though he was a bodyguard now, not a detective, he still thought like one. "She may live or work near there."

"That doesn't narrow it down much. The Seaport is only blocks away from the financial district and hundreds of companies she could be working for."

"It's not very likely that she's a broker or a trader. We could try to track her down by way of what she might be instead, but before we do that there's a much simpler place to begin. Come with me?"

Nick got up from the table. Delia hesitated before following while she looked longingly at her dinner plate.

"We'll be right back," Nick said. "We're only going to the telephone."

She did follow him then, out of the table area, past the bar to an alcove between the dining room and rest rooms. There was a pay phone on the wall. Unfortunately, there was no phone book, as is so often the case with New York City public telephones. Nick picked up the receiver. When he heard the tone begin, he dialled 4-1-1 and waited till the Information operator answered.

"Do you have a Penelope Wren in Manhattan, possibly in Lower Manhattan? And if she isn't listed, could you please check for Tobias Wren?"

Nick spelled out the last name then said what amounted to a silent prayer for the result they needed.

Maybe it was the prayer that did the trick because when the operator came back on the line she said there was, in fact, a Penelope Wren listed on Water Street.

"What street number would that be?" he asked.

Sometimes Manhattan operators got impatient with being used as an address service. Sometimes they even refused to give out that information, but Nick's prayer was apparently still in effect because this operator passed on the number he needed without so much as a hint of exasperation in her voice. Nick committed the address to memory along with the phone number that followed, from a recorded voice this time.

"Bingo," he said to Delia after he'd hung up the phone. "We've got her, and she does live in the Seaport neighborhood."

Delia smiled and nodded. "So, can we eat first before we go after her? I'm starved."

"We can definitely eat first," Nick said.

He was also thinking about some other things they could do first, when they got back to his hotel room, though he knew he shouldn't be. As he watched the dance of candlelight in Delia's eyes, Nick wondered if the search for Penelope Wren couldn't wait until tomorrow. Delia's slow smile made him wonder further if she might be feeling the same.

EVEN BEFORE they left the café, Delia had begun to think about how much she wanted to touch him. She ate much faster than was usually her habit. Of course, usually she'd be eating alone and did so slowly to stretch out the time. She did that to make each meal feel at least a little like the social event it couldn't be. Tonight was different. She cut the pâté wedges with her fork and slipped them into her mouth almost one after the other. She tasted their deep, interesting flavor only slightly. She'd ordered this dish in an automatic throwback to times past, when she'd try to eat something out of the ordinary at a meal marking a special occasion, as if that would make the experience stand out even more in her mind. Tonight, however, her special delicacy turned out to be nothing but an obstacle between herself and the delicacy she really most wanted—a private place with Nick by her side.

Probably, they should be taking off after the Wrens right now, but Delia was tired of stalking and being stalked. The cloak and dagger of these past few days had left her longing for a bit of normal human life if only for a few hours till the chase began again. She suspected Nick's diligence would make him try to convince her otherwise. She also suspected she could distract him from that resolve, at least for tonight. The truth about Tobias and Penelope Wren, whatever that might be, would still be around for the uncovering tomorrow morning.

By the time they got back to Nick's hotel room, Delia was actually feeling waves of warmth ebbing and rippling through her, like water over parched earth. She'd never been even remotely close to this filled with desire, not even five years ago when she'd first met Nick and found him so irresistible. She'd been able to keep herself under control then. She had nothing like that control now. In fact, she'd decided that if Nick put up any resistance to making love with her tonight, she'd force herself on him anyway. Fortunately, she sensed that wouldn't be necessary.

He'd matched his dining pace to hers back at the café, then snapped his fingers impatiently for the waiter when they'd finished as much of the meal as they could force themselves to eat. After that, they'd both fumbled quickly into their coats and braved the storm with mufflers still unwound. They'd hurried, down the street toward the Tivoli despite the danger of possible slippery patches under the snow, with Nick holding her firmly under the elbow against a fall.

Consequently, she wasn't surprised when Nick closed and locked the door of his room then turned and swept her into his arms, all in a single motion. They kissed— his mouth over hers, her tongue seeking his—oblivious to hats and scarves and the smell of wet wool until the heat they were generating inside their cocoons of outerwear became unbearable. They began undressing each other then, unwrapping the layers from each other's swaddled bodies with urgency, like children pulling paper from Christmas packages to get to the treasure underneath.

Nick had less on than Delia did. Still, he was making better progress. He had her coat open in no time, his fingers sliding from one button to the next like a rapid fire. Then the wet, oversize garment was off her shoulders and sliding down her arms to the floor. Almost instantly, her sweater was lifted over her head, as well. Then her turtleneck had been pulled up across her breasts. She could apply herself only sporadically to her own task of undressing him. He kept her hands and arms too busy for that. She welcomed what he was doing all the same, and not only because the air of the room felt much cooler and more soothing on her skin than the layers of humid clothing had. Even more welcome and wonderful was the way each graze of his fingers along her flesh brought with it tingles and flashes that acted like firecrackers and skyrockets in her blood, sending it crackling and surging to the most private part of her. She could barely breathe from the intensity of the sensation.

While Nick moved on to the button at the top of her jeans, Delia pulled down the zipper of his jacket. She knew she could never have managed buttons as fast as he had. Her hands were trembling too much for that, and her fingers were difficult to control, almost as if they belonged to someone else. Still she managed to force him to stop undressing her while she pushed his jacket over his shoulders, gasping at their hard roundness, then down his arms where she could feel the taut sinews even through his sweater. She set immediately to removing that sweater and the T-shirt underneath before Nick could get in her way by busying himself with her jeans once more.

As she was doing all of that, he'd begun trailing kisses down her bared and highly sensitized neck, beginning just behind her earlobe and continuing in a maddening advance toward her shoulder. She gasped at that, too, and moaned deep in her throat, so low she might have thought she imagined the sound if she hadn't felt its echo in her bones. Until his lips touched her shoulder blade and the hollow above it, Delia'd never guessed she was capable of so much feeling there. She couldn't wait to be naked against him. She reached behind her to unclasp her bra and shrugged to help him ease the straps from her shoulders. He pulled away from her just long enough to peel the pale lace from her breasts.

He might have stopped to touch her there, but that wasn't what she wanted right now. She wrapped her arms around his waist and pulled him close, crushing her breasts against his chest and moving her body just enough from side to side to feel the tantalizing torture of his dark chest hair across her nipples. Her breasts agonized for that friction, that pleasure that was almost pain, as if they must have been longing for him for years. She pressed into him farther down, as well, maneuvering her leg between his and rubbing against his groin. He raised his mouth from her throat and groaned. Under other circumstances Delia might have been taken aback, even frightened by the animal quality of that sound. Now, she reveled in its resonance with her own low moaning. She let herself go limp as Nick lifted her, seemingly without effort, into his arms and carried her to the bed.

Chapter Seventeen

The morning dawned glorious both in- and outside Nick's cozy room at the Tivoli. Delia opened the curtains to a vista of pure white rooftops sparkling in the sun. The dinginess of the city had been frosted clean overnight, and she felt the same. How could she be happy at a time like this with her life in peril and so many crucial questions remaining, not to mention the threat of imprisonment or worse forever looming? Once again, just like yesterday morning at the Waldorf, the answer lay on the bed where Nick still slept. She'd truly never met anyone like him. She probably never would again. Still she knew such thoughts must wait until her future, if she had one, could be made secure. After all, some of those crucial questions were about him. He turned toward her then as if that skeptical thought of hers might have startled him awake, or maybe it was only the sun brightening through the window.

"Good morning," he said with a sleepy smile that nearly sent her leaping across the room to him.

They'd made love several times last night. Delia felt very well-loved this morning, more so than ever before in her life. His smile reminded her of that, and all doubt about him disappeared, at least for the moment.

"Are you coming over here, or do I have to leave this warm bed and bring you back myself?"

Delia actually did a skipping step on her way across the floor. Being with him made her feel years younger, as if she hadn't lost the past five years, after all.

"We have work to do today, you know," she said as she bounced into the tumble of blankets next to him.

"We could do it later," he teased, running his finger slowly up the inside of her thigh till she trembled.

She'd found one of his blue chambray shirts in the closet and put it on. The cuffs hung winsomely past her fingertips and the tails were halfway to her knees. She'd fastened only two buttons in front, and the curve of her breasts was clearly visible almost to the nipples. She knew it was a provocative pose. She'd meant it to be, and she could tell by the heated look in Nick's eyes that he was responding as she'd hoped he would. She also knew that if they started making love now, they weren't likely to stop. The passion was that strong between them. He opened her body all the way to her soul. Her hunger burned for more of that now, but she knew she would have to wait. She pulled the chambray shirt closed with a sigh and moved her leg just in time to keep his fingers from striking the point of no return.

"Okay," he said, sounding a little pouty. "I get the message. But—" he raised himself up on one gorgeously muscled arm and swept her down onto the bed with the other "—you're not getting away without a kiss."

And what a kiss it was. He rolled on top of her with his thighs between hers so she could feel every inch of his magnificent, naked body pressing into hers. He lifted her against him with one arm, crushing her breasts to his chest. His other hand cradled her head and held her while his mouth captured hers and his tongue invaded her so forcefully that she couldn't have resisted if she wanted to. Of course, she had no intention of resisting. She threw her arms around him and returned his almost savage kiss with equal hot, hard intensity. When they finally pulled away from each other, Delia lay out of breath in his arms. If he hadn't been the one to get up finally and say they'd better get going, she would have tossed her former resolve straight out into the snow and loved this amazing man all day long.

NICK HAD WANTED to keep Delia in his room this morning just so he could be alone with her, but there'd been another reason, too. He still possessed a cop's instincts, and those instincts were telling him loud and clear that she could be in great danger in the day ahead, even more than she was now. That's why he did his best to talk her into staying at the Tivoli. Unfortunately, he hadn't succeeded.

He could understand why she felt she had to come out here this morning, why she couldn't hang out in bed with him instead. She had a mystery on her hands, a mystery that had just about consumed her life for years. If there was even a hint of a possibility she could unlock a single one of the closed doors to the puzzle of her past, she had to take that chance. And he had to take it with her, even when this sixth sense of his was telling him to grab her and run. So they'd left the Tivoli and plowed out into the snow, through sidewalks that were half shoveled or not shoveled at all. With each step they took, the warning alarms buzzed louder in Nick's head. Yet, now that they were here outside the building on Water Street where Penelope Wren lived, all of that noise inside Nick had fallen silent. He felt nothing but dead calm.

Developers had obviously been at work on this block. Eighteenth-century row houses that had fallen into disrepair a decade or so ago were fixed up now, with repointed and cleaned brick fronts. Restored window casings sprouted planter boxes on the ledges, filled with snow where flowers would be in a warmer season. Christmas lights were strung along the edges of some of the boxes and more in the windows. Nick looked up as they mounted the stoop and saw that the Christmas lights in the third-floor windows were lit even in the morning brightness. Something told him those lights weren't on due to the occupant's excess of holiday spirit the evening before. Something also told him that third-floor apartment belonged to Penelope Wren. The mailbox in the entryway confirmed that intuition to be true.

Delia grabbed the front door handle and turned it in vain, then turned it again. Nick could tell how eager she was to get inside and on to whatever revelation this building had in store, no matter how unpleasant Nick might anticipate it to be. He could protect her. It was his job to do that, and more than just his job now. He could jump in front of her and take danger and even destruction on himself so it wouldn't strike her. But he couldn't shield her from the truth. He might pick her up in his arms right now and carry her out of here as fast as he could go, but he couldn't hold on to her like that forever. Eventually she'd make her way back here despite any and all efforts of his to prevent it. Facing the reality of this building, including its third floor, was inevitable for both of them.

"The door's locked," he said, though that was already obvious.

He knew, of course, that Delia wasn't about to be stopped by something as trivial as a lock. She turned back to the row of mailboxes in the entryway. There was a door buzzer under each. She hesitated a moment before pushing one then another. Checking the name plates and apartment numbers for those two buttons, Nick could see what Delia was trying to do. She was hoping to ring the buzzers of apartments at the rear of the building. That way nobody would lean out the window to see who was down here. There was no response for a moment. Then a voice crackled through the intercom grill set into the same brass facing as the row of mailboxes.

"Who's there?" The voice was hardly recognizable as male or female.

When Delia didn't answer right away, Nick chimed in. "Mailman," he said.

He knew he was helping Delia do something he thought unwise, but he'd already surrendered to the inevitability of the situation. Still, he held his breath, hoping the person attached to that crackling voice would be savvy enough not to let somebody into his or her building on the strength of such a flimsy identification. At the same time Nick guessed that his mailman charade would work. Too many people were too eager to find out what was being delivered to resist that particular temptation, especially at Christmastime. A moment later the door release buzzer sounded and he and Delia were inside.

"We'd better get upstairs fast before whoever that was opens their door," Delia said.

She was already at the stairway to the first floor and climbing. Nick shrugged and followed. They hotfooted up to the first landing then down a narrow hallway to the next staircase. He kept close behind her up the next flight of stairs and back down the third floor hallway toward the front of the building again. Not till he saw the doorway of that front apartment did he grab Delia's arm and thrust her out of his way so he could approach first. She didn't resist, maybe because she'd seen the same thing he had and understood his concern. The door to the third floor front apartment was ajar. In New York City, an unlocked and open door to a residential space like this one more often than not signaled trouble.

Delia tapped Nick on the arm. "Take this," she said.

He turned from staring at the crack in the doorway just long enough to see that she was handing him the gun he'd given her yesterday. He shook his head and took his own weapon from the back of his waistband. She did understand that there was danger, after all.

"You stay out here," he said softly, hoping in vain that she would cooperate for once.

He raised his gun next to his face and slightly forward in quick-response position, then pressed his left palm flat against the apartment door and pushed. He peered at the space revealed by the gradually opening door, but could see nothing unusual. He pushed the door open wider. Still nothing. Both the hallway into the apartment and the room beyond were brightly illuminated, and that made him as uneasy as the Christmas bulbs in the third-floor window had done.

He motioned for Delia to stay put while he darted across the space in front of the open doorway to the opposite side. He peered through into the apartment from this new angle. Again, he saw nothing suspicious.

"Are you going in?" Delia whispered.

Nick signaled her to be silent, then nodded. He was definitely going in. He had no choice. He remembered experiences like this one back when he was a cop. This moment outside the door to possible danger was the longest and scariest of all. That was one reason for making the entrance fast, like ripping off an adhesive bandage before you could think too much about how much it was going to hurt. Nick took a deep breath and wished he didn't sense that Delia was right behind him.

DELIA WASN'T about to stay in the hallway. She had to know what was going on here. She followed Nick as he crept along the hallway wall. She couldn't help but be impressed by how formidable, even deadly, he looked with that gun in his hand. She could all but see every muscle in his body, tense as steel and on the verge of a spring-to-action at the slightest provocation. If there was peril in one of these rooms, Nick was obviously ready. It occurred to her that he would have been a real asset to PEI all these years she'd kept him off her roster of operatives. Maybe all of that could change now. Yet she didn't feel comfortable thinking in terms of the future where Nick was concerned. She still had too many questions about him for that.

The question of the moment concerned why he was taking so many precautions now. The total silence suggested that there was nobody in this apartment but the two of them. As they passed one empty room after another, his military-alert pose began to appear a little dramatic. Delia was tempted to rush on ahead of him to confirm her suspicion that they were entirely alone here. Then she could get down to searching for anything she might find out about Penelope and Tobias Wren—what they were doing in New York, how long they'd been here, what their connection was to the events of these past few days. In fact, a search might turn up more such information than a face-to-face interview with the Wrens ever could. For that reason Delia was almost glad to find the place empty. Then they got to the bathroom.

The first sign of trouble was a smudge, so small Delia would later wonder why she'd even noticed it right off like she did. The mark was on the edge of the door just above the lock plate, and in the dimmed light from the hallway she couldn't even see what color it was. Her heart started thumping anyway, even before Nick eased the door open and they both saw what waited inside. Penelope Wren was on the floor, halfway in and halfway out of the bathtub, as if she might have been trying to crawl in there to escape her terrible fate.

Suddenly, for Delia, it was five years ago and she had just awakened to find poor Morty Lancer's body cold and dead next to her in her bed. All she could think about was getting out of there. She stepped away from the bathroom door and slammed her back against the opposite wall so hard one of the pictures was shaken from its hook and fell to the floor with a shattering sound. Delia didn't look at the picture or more than peripherally register its fall. She was riveted on Penelope and Nick leaning over her body, taking her pulse, listening for her heartbeat. How useless all of that was. There is nothing as still as the stillness of death. Delia had never had that thought before or even realized it was true, but she did so now. She didn't need to lift Penelope's wrist or listen to her chest to know without the tiniest shadow of a doubt that the woman would never stand up from that floor on her own again.

''She's dead,'' Nick said.

Delia wanted to shout, I know. I know. You don't need to tell me.

She stood silent instead, pressed against the wall, wishing she could dissolve into and through it and be out of here. The doorway beckoned. Down the hall, just a few yards and she'd be gone. She'd clean out her accounts and be on a plane leaving the country before even Nick could catch up to her. Maybe that's what she should have done five years ago, left the country altogether. Mexico, the Islands, maybe Greece—didn't Greece have some kind of nonextradition policy? Of course, that probably didn't include murder. All of these thoughts and more raced through her head in the seconds it took for Nick to rise from where he'd been crouched on one knee next to Penelope.

Delia knew that if he turned around and she saw his face, she'd be lost. She could never run away, with him watching her, and with all she felt about him no matter how conflicted it might be, beckoning her to stay. She let her panicky thoughts of flight pass. Maybe that was a decision to stay and face whatever came next. Maybe it was a failure to make any decision at all. Either way, when he turned toward her she was still pressed against the wall. She gazed up into his eyes and sought sanctuary there, but he looked as stricken as she felt.

"We should get out of here," he said. "There's nothing we can do for her now, and I don't want you involved."

He was already checking out ways to cover any tracks they might be leaving behind, wiping the doorknob and the edge of the door where he'd put his hand. She could tell he was being careful not to remove the smudge.

"I don't want to leave just yet," she said.

"The police could be on their way here right now."

Nick's tone was urgent, and he sounded determined. Delia was determined, too.

"I have to see what I can find," she said. "Besides, it looks like we're the first people to have been here since... it happened."

She turned away from the bathroom doorway and started toward the other rooms of the apartment. She didn't like to think about what "it" had been.

"By the way," Nick said from close behind her, "I would say she died sometime last evening."

Delia was almost to the archway that led into the living room when she caught on to the significance of that.

"I saw Penelope last night," Delia said.

"Yes, I know you did."

Delia spun around to face him. "I didn't kill her if that's what you're implying."

Her voice was choked, and she was right on the edge of breaking down. She held her body tense, as if to keep herself from toppling over that edge.

"I've never killed anybody in my life," she said, still choking the words out that had to be said, for last night and for five years ago.

"I know that."

"Do you?"

He didn't answer right away. Something in his eyes, or maybe something that wasn't in his eyes, told her what he'd said was almost true. But not entirely. She turned and continued into the living room, moving much faster than before.

"Delia, listen to me."

Nick was behind her with his hands on her shoulders. There was pleading in the way he'd asked her to listen. She couldn't succumb to that, not yet anyway.

"No," she said sharply, and jerked herself out of his grasp. "I have to search."

"For what?"

Delia was suddenly struck by how hysterically funny a question that was, so much so, she almost started laughing. What did she have to search for? The meaning of her life? The answers to death? The impossibility of her position made everything absurd somehow, and eerie, too, like the flickering reflection of the Christmas lights flashing off and on from the window. What could she expect to find here that would tear down the mountain of suspicions against her, the lingering doubts in Nick's mind? Now she'd be considered a prime suspect in Penelope's murder as well as poor Morty's. Delia had the motive. She'd had the opportunity, too, since she was only blocks from this place last night. This was beginning to feel very déjà vu indeed.

Delia set herself to searching, rummaging through drawers mostly, hoping she'd know what she was looking for when she found it. That turned out to be exactly the case when she got to the lap drawer of the desk near the window with the Christmas lights. Delia found a letter there from, of all people, her brother Samuel. Before she'd even read the contents, she knew this was about as important a clue to what had been happening to her and around her as there could possibly be.

Chapter Eighteen

"What's that?" Nick asked, nodding toward the envelope and two pages of closely written stationery in her hand.

Delia couldn't answer just yet. She was still too stunned. She'd been astonished enough to find a communication from the older brother who'd virtually disappeared from their family years ago. Then she saw the return address on the envelope, and true shock set in. According to this letter, Samuel was living right here in Manhattan, on the Upper West Side near Riverside Park. Delia's first thought, when she was once again able to think, was that Samuel might have been dumped up there in the kind of institution bailout that had sent so many poor, stricken souls back to the city streets whether they were mentally equipped to cope there or not. The Upper West Side had become a chief wandering zone for many such unfortunates. But why wouldn't the Lester money have shielded Samuel from such a fate? She'd been out of touch with the family too long to know the answer to that.

"Delia, is something wrong?"

She looked up at Nick as if she might have forgotten he was present, though that was only partly true.

"It's a letter from my brother," she said.

"Samuel?"

"Yes." It sometimes slipped her mind that Nick's history with her family meant he knew a lot about them, even the sad story of Samuel. "You would never have met him, but I'm sure you heard about him."

"I met him. I knew him pretty well, in fact."

Delia was gazing at the letter, though she hadn't yet read beyond the first sentence. She was wondering if she could bring herself to read farther when Nick's words jolted her attention back to him.

"That can't be true," she said. "You couldn't have met him. You must be thinking of somebody else."

"It is true. I used to take your father to see Samuel, once a week or so."

Delia remembered her father's visits to Samuel all too well. She'd tried not to resent them when she was in her teens, but she couldn't help it. She didn't like to think of her beloved dad having such a close relationship with someone who made no pretense of wishing her nothing but harm. Samuel had made it very clear that he hated her. That was one of the reasons he'd been institutionalized when she was still an infant. He'd tried so many times to hurt her that he'd finally had to be put away. She understood how his addled mind saw her as the enemy taking over his territory. Unfortunately, understanding that had never kept her from feeling the hurt of having a brother who wished she'd never been born.

"Samuel and I even got to be friends," Nick was saying. "As much as that was possible for him, anyway."

"You liked him?"

Delia could feel some of that old resentment. Here was another man in her life professing affection for this person she'd grown up thinking of as a scary monster. If there was a single, consistent image in her nightmares from those years, that image was of Samuel.

"Yes, I liked him. He needed friends from outside the rest home. Your father felt strongly about that. I was one of the few opportunities Samuel had for a friendship like that to happen."

"It wasn't a rest home," Delia said, sounding more at ease with the subject than she felt. "That's a term the family used to cover up the truth. He was in a mental institution."

"Whatever."

Nick was watching her warily, as if he could hear what lay beneath her surface calm, as if he might think she was about to explode. She could see that attitude in his eyes, and it made her more agitated than ever and less able to keep that agitation under control.

"Whatever?" she said. "Whatever Samuel needed, it was not rest. They locked him up in that place, supposedly for life, so he wouldn't hurt anybody when he flew into one of his violent rages. Now—" she brandished the letter in front of Nick's face "—now, he's out."

"I don't believe it."

"See for yourself."

Nick took the envelope out of her hand. She watched as he looked it over, including the return address.

"From this, what you say appears to be true," he said.

"It's true, all right. He's out of that institution and living in Manhattan. What do you think about that?"

Nick shook his head slowly. He continued to examine the envelope until she took it out of his hand.

"I asked what you think of my emotionally disturbed brother Samuel being right here in Manhattan."

"I don't know exactly what to think. I would have said he was too sick to be released from the hospital, at least back when I knew him."

"Well, I'd say that his being here could explain a lot of things."

Nick studied her for a moment. "What things?"

"Things like what's been happening to me these past few days."

"You mean the fact that someone's been stalking you and trying to run you down? You think Samuel could be the stalker?"

"No," she admitted. "I've seen the color of that man's eyes, and I know he's not Samuel. But my brother *is* mentally disturbed, isn't he? He could have hired it done. Unlike me, he has his share of his inheritance, even if he has somebody managing it for him. He must have some access. With even a fraction of the Lester money at his disposal, he could afford to have anything done to anybody. Not to mention the fact that he's always hated me. Did you know that?"

"I heard about it," Nick said in a guarded tone.

Delia wondered if this was the way Nick used to talk to Samuel, as if he had to be handled with kid gloves because he might go off the deep end otherwise. That possibility didn't please her at all.

"I heard a lot of things from Samuel," Nick was saying. "He didn't necessarily mean any of them."

"Did he mean the threats of the terrible things he'd do to me if he ever had the chance?"

"I don't think so," Nick said, but he didn't sound altogether certain of that. He paused a moment. "I don't know," he amended more quietly. "He was a troubled guy, and he desperately didn't want to be. He was angry with you for being normal."

"That certainly wraps him up in a neat little package. Meanwhile, I'm the one who's being terrorized."

Nick looked at her for a moment without speaking. "That's right," he said finally. "You are." He sounded sad. "You're the one being terrorized, and Penelope Wren is the one who's dead."

Penelope had slipped from Delia's mind when Samuel's letter turned up. She could hardly believe she'd stopped thinking about a woman who had once taken care of her and was now a corpse on the bathroom floor. What was this situation making Delia into? She didn't know if she could face the answer to that, at least not right now.

"Let's get out of here," she said, and headed for the door to the outside hallway.

"Where are we going?" Nick asked.

She waved the letter and envelope where he could see them. "We're going to follow up on this."

DELIA INSISTED on taking a cab uptown to the West Side. It was a long ride to make in total silence. Nick's practice in the past had been to keep himself at a distance from some of the more convoluted aspects of the Lester family saga. Samuel was an exception to that rule. He was maybe the most lonely person Nick had ever met in his life, shut away in that gilded cage of a high-priced lockup and doomed to spend his entire life there, or so it was supposedly planned. Edward Lester understood his son's sorrowful solitude and was heartbroken for him. That had been painfully obvious in the many long, silent trips back from those visits to Samuel. Nick would drive while Mr. Lester stared out the window, lost in a sorrowful solitude of his own. Tears rose in his eyes more than once after his visits to his son. Nick had seen them there and respectfully glanced away.

Sorrowful or not, however, there was never any question that Samuel belonged exactly where he was. Without question, he was dangerous, but contrary to his ravings and Delia's fears, he had never in his life hurt anyone other than himself. Whatever the source might be of Samuel's psychotic rage, he was the sole victim. That was the primary reason he needed constant custodial care. That was the reason Edward Lester could never bring his son home, no matter how much he longed to do so. Even medication only halted Samuel's self-destruction temporarily. Still, he'd never struck out at those around him, even those whose job it was to restrain and imprison him. That was why Nick found it hard to believe Samuel was responsible for terrorizing Delia. That was why the possibility of Samuel as her stalker had never entered Nick's mind. Besides, Nick had understood that Samuel had been locked up with no chance of release.

But that wasn't what troubled Nick most and kept him staring out his own side of the cab through this long ride made longer by streets narrowed to single lanes bordered in banks of snow. He wasn't even most concerned with what might be waiting for them at the address on the envelope Delia had waved in his face, then had torn away. He was most unsettled of all by Delia herself and the deep sadness he'd seen in her eyes when she spoke of Samuel, deep sadness mixed with what he guessed to be carefully controlled rage. If he was right about that, what could her repressed anger make her capable of if it suddenly slipped its bonds? Could she, after all, have been the one who killed Mortimer Lancer? Could she have the cold heart of a murderer? He knew she could be stubborn, but he had never known her to be hard-hearted. In fact, it was the very softness of her heart, so obvious to him beneath the guard of her defenses, that had drawn him to her in the first place and continued to draw him—until now. Could he have been wrong about her all along? The possibility plagued him, block after block, all the way to Ninety-first Street.

Riverside Park was a blanket of white, and Nick found himself reminded of Denver yet again. The buildings here were mostly what they call prewar and often divided into much larger apartments than was otherwise the case in Manhattan. Nick had been in some of those apartments in the course of his work. They were pretty nice. Maybe Samuel *was* living well. Still, Nick couldn't imagine Samuel on his own. Maybe he was being taken care of by a family in a private home situation, or there could be a group hostel up here somewhere. There was also always the possibility of Samuel having undergone a miraculous cure, but somehow Nick didn't think that was the case.

He wished he'd been able to read the letter Delia found. She'd stuffed it into her pocket before he could do much more than peruse the envelope to see if the handwriting looked familiar. He'd seen some pages in Samuel's journal once, and the envelope could possibly be in the same hand. Nick couldn't be sure, and he didn't want to ask Delia to let him examine it again. He could feel her sadness, deeper even than before, filling the cab. He respected that sadness and her silence and left her to herself.

Samuel's address turned out to be a building with a doorman. He asked their destination, and Delia gave the apartment number from Samuel's letter. When the doorman asked who he should say was calling, she answered, "Penelope Wren," without so much as a flutter of her long lashes. Once again Nick was struck by how expertly she lied. It bothered him to see her do that even in a good cause like this one. Honesty was something he put a high value on. Meanwhile he held his breath to see what would happen when the doorman called up to Samuel's apartment with the news that Penelope Wren was supposedly downstairs.

The doorman turned back from the phone on the wall and smiled. "Go right up," he said.

"Thank you." Delia smiled back at him. No one would ever have guessed that she'd just identified herself as a woman who lay murdered on a bathroom floor a few miles away.

Nick had stopped to make an anonymous call to the police before hailing the cab to bring them uptown. The detectives would have arrived at Penelope Wren's apartment by now. Nick mentally reviewed the places he'd wiped to remove his fingerprints and Delia's. He thought he got them all, but he wasn't a hundred percent sure. He was worrying over that small chance of error as the elevator moved upward. Delia stood in front of him, maintaining her silence. She didn't have to speak to tell him how tense she was. He could see it in the rigid set of her shoulders. She was as anxious as he was about what they would find on the eleventh floor.

What they did find was another unlocked door with a yellow note stuck to it. "Penelope—Come on in," the note said in a scrawl that could have been Samuel's.

Delia had her hand on the doorknob when Nick reached out and took her arm.

"Let me go first," he said. He already had his gun out.

"I guess that's necessary?" she asked, looking at the weapon.

"Yes, it is."

She gazed up at him for a moment, then took her hand off the knob and stepped aside with a resigned sigh. She had to know that even if there was only Samuel on the other side of this door, and even if Nick was right about her brother posing no real danger to anybody, erring on the side of caution was always best. Still, Nick could understand why she might not want her first meeting with her brother in many, many years to begin at gunpoint. Nick had his weapon at the ready all the same as he turned the doorknob slowly, then eased the door open inch by inch, just as he had at Penelope's place.

What greeted them inside could hardly have been more disarming. The splashing shower was clearly audible from down the hall into the interior of the apartment, and above that, the sound of singing. A tuneless ditty it was, unrecognizable and quite loud, the kind of thing a nonsinger belts out in the shower for the fun of it when nobody is around to hear. Nick looked back over his shoulder at Delia, and she returned his glance. Some release of tension was obvious from her expression. Nick, on the other hand, wasn't ready to relax just yet.

The apartment was the kind he'd like to live in himself if he were a permanent New Yorker. The ceilings were high, probably ten feet, and the living room was large with an archway into an only slightly smaller dining area. The walls of the living room were covered with paintings from waist height up. Delia was studying the paintings with a curious expression on her face.

"Quite a collection," Nick remarked.

"Yes." She sounded lost in thought as she wandered along one side of the room and examined the pieces above an artfully faded burgundy velvet sofa.

"What do you think?"

She turned to look at him. The curiosity in her eyes had turned to something deeper, as if she might be trying to figure out a perturbing problem.

"I think I'm impressed," she said.

"I get the feeling that I've seen paintings like these before. Not the same ones, but something like them. I just can't remember where it was."

"My father's study," she said. Her voice seemed to come from somewhere far off. "You saw a collection very much like this one in my father's study."

She was right. Her father did have his study walls crammed with paintings, just like these were, paintings of a similar style, as well.

"Do you see any of your father's paintings here?" Nick asked. "Would you remember if you did?"

"I'd remember all right. That study was my favorite room in the house. I spent a lot of time there looking at those walls."

Now that she mentioned it, Nick did remember her disappearing into her father's study for hours at a time. She probably would recognize if these were the same pictures. Nick was relieved to hear that they weren't. There were already more than enough mysteries to deal with in this situation.

"So, what do you think?" she asked him, as he had asked her moments before.

"I'm not sure I know what to think."

"Don't tell me you're not asking yourself the same question I'm asking myself."

"What question is that?"

She turned and walked toward him across the Oriental carpet that covered the center of the floor.

"The question I'm asking myself," she said, "is whether I actually believe this art collection could belong to my brother Samuel."

Nick thought about that for a moment.

"Well, Samuel and your father spent a lot of time together. Maybe they talked about art some of that time. Maybe your father taught him things."

"Everything I ever heard about Samuel's mental condition would suggest he'd have a lot of trouble taking in anything so complex as the principles of creating an art collection."

"But that was back then. We don't know what could have happened to Samuel in between."

She was standing in front of Nick now, studying his face much like she'd just been studying the paintings on the walls of this graciously sedate room.

"That's right," she said. "We don't know what's happened to him in between." She sighed and looked away from Nick's face, toward the tall windows overlooking the Hudson River.

Nick couldn't see her face, but he could hear the wistful sadness in her voice. Nick felt a pang in his heart for her. Still, he couldn't help wondering yet again how much of what he saw in Delia now was really and truly her and how much was the person she'd made up to show the world.

"Maybe Samuel found a miracle." Nick spoke tenderly despite his doubts about her.

"Maybe."

She cleared her throat and turned abruptly back toward him. He could see her recomposing herself, snapping herself back into the carefully controlled woman she was anytime other than when they were making love.

"Let's have a look at the other rooms," she said.

She swept past him before he could take hold of her and maybe even pull her into his arms. Nick was the one to sigh this time. Then he remembered what he should have been thinking about all along. He was supposed to be in the lead. They had no idea what they were going to run into here. He could still hear the shower, more loudly now that they were back out in the hallway again. The enthusiastic singing had stopped. Even so, Nick had to admit this didn't seem like a very dangerous place. Probably the guy's voice gave out. How long can anybody sing at the top of their lungs, anyway?

Still, Delia shouldn't be out front like she was with Nick tagging along. He'd let his distractions into the way he felt about her make him forget his job again. He hurried after her, but she'd already turned into a doorway to the left just past the dining room. She didn't even hesitate so much as an instant to check the interior of the room before walking in. That was a surefire way to get caught in an ambush. Nick cursed under his breath and brought his gun to ready position once more. When he got to the doorway she'd entered, he held himself back from dashing in there even though he wanted to. If she was in trouble, he wouldn't be much help if he went barreling into danger right along with her.

Nick backed himself against the wall and took a deep breath to focus himself. He edged closer to the doorway and very gradually peeked around into the room. Delia was alone in what looked to be somebody's study. She was in the midst of a slow, visual sweep of the walls. She turned gradually as she looked, appearing to examine each new angle in great detail until finally she was facing the doorway and Nick standing there watching her. He'd lowered the gun to his side, but her eyes found it there immediately.

"Please, put that away," she said.

He might have protested that they were in unfamiliar territory here, but what he saw in her eyes kept him from doing that. He tucked the gun into the back of his belt instead and took a step toward her. He hadn't entirely understood that he was about to take her into his arms until she spoke again. She waved her hand in front of her first, as if to draw a line in front of her. "Don't" was all she said, but he could see instantly what she meant. She needed not to be touched right now. What he didn't comprehend was why. The bewilderment in her eyes told him he had to find out.

"What's going on?" he asked.

"That's what I want to know." Her voice was trembling. "That's what I *have* to know."

"About what?" He could barely stand to see her this way without being close enough to comfort her.

She swept her arm around in a circle to indicate the room without looking back at it.

"About this?"

Nick followed the direction of her gesture. It took a minute to sink in, but then he saw what she was talking about. The imprint of her father's taste was everywhere. Nick could see that more readily here because of the hours he'd spent in Edward Lester's study all those years ago in Colorado. Suddenly, Nick understood what

Delia was feeling. He felt some of it himself, as if he'd been transported back to a better, happier time only to be slapped in the face with the reminder that this better time was gone forever.

Nick moved into the room then, despite her having asked him not to. She was moving, too, turned away from him and walking toward the desk at the opposite end of the room in front of a window onto Riverside Park and the morning. Nick followed, reaching out toward her. He wanted to hold her, however hard she might resist, until she was quiet in his arms. He wanted to make her feel safe there, from the sadness of the past and the uncertainty of the present. At the moment nothing could matter to him more—which would explain why he didn't see what else was happening in that room till it was too late to be prepared for it.

Chapter Nineteen

For a wonderful and terrible moment, Delia thought it was her father bursting through the glass doors from the dining area into the study. His presence was so much with her in this room filled with books like those he'd read, furniture in his particular taste, objects he would love, that she'd half expected him to walk in even before the rattle of glass and slamming open of the double doors announced an arrival. Then she saw those eyes, in a flash only, as they glinted at her on the way to their true target. It was the man who'd stalked her from her office and tried to assault her at the Waldorf Hotel, but she wasn't his intended victim this morning, at least not his first intended victim. He was after Nick.

The initial onslaught happened so fast she could barely register what was going on. The man with the burning eyes crashed into the room and was on top of Nick in an instant. She saw the attacker reach behind Nick. In seconds, he was brandishing the gun Nick had had in the waistband of his jeans. In another flash, both men had their hands on the weapon as they each struggled for possession. All Delia could think of was how she'd told Nick to put the gun away, and if she hadn't done that he wouldn't be in so much danger now. The pain of that thought thudded into the pit of her stomach. Then she heard a loud clatter and her prayers were answered. The gun was out of the attacker's hand and sliding across the floor.

Of course, that meant the gun was out of Nick's hands as well. They were fighting unarmed, grabbing at each other and trying to land punches that mostly half connected as they shoved from one side of the room to the other, toppling a chair and jarring books from the shelves.

Delia was struck by how different the smoothly choreographed fight scenes in movies were from the real thing. She also didn't intend to be like the women in some of those films who stood around and shrieked while a man battled on her behalf. Delia would do her part, too. She had a weapon of her own. Or so she thought. She felt in her coat pocket for the Beretta, but it wasn't there. Maybe it had dropped from her pocket during their ride in the cab. Whatever might have happened, the gun was gone, and she needed to find the one Nick and his attacker had just let go of.

She'd heard it bounce along the floor in the general direction of the doorway to the hall. She'd have to make her way past the two grappling men to get there. She waited what seemed like forever for them to move out of her path. She had begun to brush past them when a hand snaked out of nowhere and clamped onto her forearm. She knew instantly that this hand didn't belong to Nick. He would never touch her so roughly or growl at her as his opponent in combat was doing now. Her reaction was instantaneous.

"Take your hands off me," she shouted, and there was a growl in her voice, too.

She balled her free hand into a fist and began pounding at his wrist. Instinctively she knew that would be the weakest area of his grip. She pounded with all her strength and all her anger, and none of her blows failed to connect with their mark. He gripped tighter at first. Then, as she continued to punish his wrist, she could feel that grip slacken. In the meantime he also had only one arm and fist free with which to fight off Nick. It occurred to Delia, in one of those flashes of understanding that can come at the most unlikely times, that whoever this guy was he must have thought she was making an escape out the door when he grabbed her. He had to want to keep her from leaving in the worst way or he wouldn't have made himself so vulnerable to Nick.

The consequences of that action were swift and certain. Delia felt as much as saw the fast-rising arc of Nick's right arm. That arm then descended in a flash of motion and didn't miss its target this time. Nick socked his opponent so hard that the shock of the impact shook Delia, as well. Suddenly the grasp on her was gone. Instantly she was at the doorway, crouched over and searching the floor for Nick's gun. She didn't see it anywhere. Could it have slid far enough to travel through the doorway into the hall?

She was about to dash out there for a look when she noticed the chair that had been shoved askew in the struggle that was still going on despite the punch she'd hoped would be decisive in Nick's favor. The chair rested against the bookcase with one leg knocked up onto the bottom shelf. It was that kiltered angle that had kept Delia from noticing the gun. She dove for the chair so fast she almost struck her head on the lamp table next to it. She did manage to knock the lamp to the floor with a crash.

The two men at the other side of the room both glanced in her direction for an instant. Nick's attacker must have figured out what she had in mind to do because he tried to get away from Nick in a hard lunge, probably to grab her again. She could see Nick straining not to break his hold. This guy with the crazy eyes was a fierce fighter even against somebody as powerful as Nick. She was sure Nick would win out in the end, but it looked like he'd have to take a painful beating on the way to that victory. Delia wasn't going to let that happen. She reached under the chair and felt for the gun. She all but cried out with joy when her fingers touched it. She was back on her feet in a flash with the gun gripped in both hands and pointed just as she'd seen Nick do.

"You can take your hands off him now," she shouted.

Once again the men halted their fevered wrestling to look in her direction. In that instant she saw those crazy eyes more clearly than ever. Their maniacal gleam blazed into her as if they had the power to send her into flames and their owner was willing them to do just that. A shudder of fear rocketed through her. Suddenly she understood that she was gazing into the face of not just craziness but evil, as well. Her breath caught in her throat so hard she couldn't exhale. For the second time that day, all she wanted to do was run. She'd run out of this study that reminded her of her father. She'd run out of this building she wished she had never come to. Most of all, she would run away from these eyes that were telling her as clearly as if they had voice how much she was in danger of harm.

Nick, still straining to hold on to his enemy, managed a nod in her direction. She knew that was a signal for her to act. He needed her help, and he needed it now. Five years of relentlessly tuned escape instincts struggled with that need and her response to it as violently as these two men were struggling. Then she saw Nick's eyes, so different from that other pair. Nick's eyes were dark and fathoms deep. They beckoned her, and that beckoning reached through her fear. In the shadowed light of her lover's eyes, she found her courage once again.

"I said let go of him," she shouted. "Let go of him or I'll shoot you."

She meant that, even though she'd never physically harmed another human being in her life and could not have imagined herself doing so before this moment. She knew she could shoot this man now and deal with how she'd feel about it later. He must have known that, too, because he backed away from Nick, only a step at first, then farther as she motioned with the barrel of the gun for him to do so. The man let go of Nick. Delia had to force herself to look into the attacker's disturbing eyes. Otherwise he might doubt her resolve to do him as much damage, if necessary, as he longed to do her.

Nick was at her side the instant he was released. He put his hand over hers with the gun in it. She didn't let go. An impulse more basic than reason had clamped this weapon into her grip and refused to give ground now for anyone. If she'd stopped to describe what that steel-hard resolve felt like, she would have called it primitive. This was about survival, as surely as all combat against a sworn enemy had ever been, and she was determined to prevail. Nick tugged at her grip on the gun once more.

"I'll take it now," he said, close to her ear and still a little out of breath.

"No," she said. She'd been breathless, too, a moment ago. Now she was as calm and steady as the rock hardness of her resolve. "Find something to tie him up with, then we'll get out of here."

Nick kept his hand on hers a moment longer.

"I can handle this," she said, and she knew she could. "Please, just tie him up now."

Nick must have heard both the determination and the pleading in those words because he let go of her hand and reached for the lamp she'd knocked to the floor when she was going for the gun. The lamp cord had been pulled out of the wall socket. He picked up the lamp in one hand and wrapped the cord around the fist of the other. He gave the cord a mighty yank and snapped it free of the lamp base. He hurried to the other man's side and forced his hands behind his back. Minutes later Nick had his attacker trussed up tight.

Delia waited till Nick had preceded her out of the study door. Then she backed out of the room still pointing the gun at the man who lay so supposedly helpless on the floor. Craziness and evil had been subdued, but only for the moment. He would be back after her again probably very soon. She was sure of that. Still, she couldn't bring herself to put the pressure on her trigger finger that would have put an end to that probability. Instead she turned and ran after Nick down the hallway toward at least momentary escape.

NICK DIDN'T TRY to talk to Delia right away. He could tell by her eyes that he shouldn't. They were set and staring, almost as if she might be walking in her sleep. She'd been through so much these past few days and even more this morning. He would have liked to take her in his arms and hold her tight so she'd know she was safe, but gently so she'd know he cared. He did care, more than he could remember ever caring. At least for right now he wouldn't let himself think about how many doubts and problems came with allowing this particular woman inside his heart. He only let himself think about how much she needed him and how much he wanted to fill those needs.

All the same, he didn't take her in his arms or even stand very close to her in the elevator ride back to street level. She was giving off clearly discernible signals that she'd gone off into an isolated part of herself and didn't want anyone to follow. He understood that she needed this solitude for her mind to adjust to the shattering blows of just these past few hours—discovery of a body on a bathroom floor, attack by a crazed man—not to mention five years of constant tension and uncertainty. That could put anybody in the way of needing some downtime. He left her alone because of that. Besides, she still had the gun.

They were by themselves in the elevator. Nick didn't say anything about the drawn weapon she held in the hand hanging at her side. When they walked through the lobby, he edged close enough to block any view of what she was carrying. He cast what he suspected might look like a nervous smile in the doorman's direction. If the man noticed anything at all peculiar in that, he was too well trained in discretion to let it show. When Nick and Delia were finally outside, he breathed a sigh that sent a cloud of vapor into the cold, crisp air.

He turned left and, fortunately, she followed, out from under the building's awning and away from that area of visibility through the glass front doors. He waited till they were well away from that entrance before moving off from the center of the sidewalk into the lee of another building where they'd be less conspicuous. He mentally crossed his fingers that she'd follow. He breathed another cloud of vapor when she did. She turned with him as if there were a string attached from his shoulder to hers and she'd been programmed to take her cues from any tug on that connection.

"You can give me the gun now," he said in a carefully even tone.

She looked up at him, raising her eyes slowly from their straight ahead stare to his face. He didn't detect any of what he would call recognition there at first. She'd merely transferred her blank stare to a new target.

"I'd like you to give the gun to me now," he said.

He continued to betray no hint of urgency though he knew exactly how urgent it in fact was to get that gun away from her in her present, unpredictable state. Meanwhile he thought he might have seen a flicker of something in her eyes, but maybe he only wished it would be there.

"Delia, it's me. Nick."

"I know who you are."

Her answer was so unexpected he almost jumped at the sound. He had to remind himself not to make any startling moves.

"I thought you wanted this," she said.

She was holding the gun in front of her and toward him. He reached carefully across the space between them, still taking extra care not to do anything alarming, especially while the gun was pointed at his midsection. He touched the gun barrel first and eased its aim gradually outward toward the currently empty street. He slipped his fingers over hers on the grip and was about to say something he hoped would coax her to let go. She did so all of a sudden then, without being asked. Fortunately, Nick's instincts were keener than he might have expected after so much stress and strain. He clamped his fingers around the gun before it could clatter down onto the sidewalk.

"I'm hungry," she said as matter-of-factly as if they were out for nothing more than a morning, or actually by now midday, stroll. "There's a diner not far from here on Broadway."

She turned away from him without another word and began walking east on Ninety-first Street.

Chapter Twenty

They were seated in a booth at the Argo Restaurant before Delia came fully back to herself. She'd ordered a hearty breakfast though it was well past breakfast time. She wanted the comfort a steaming plate of eggs scrambled soft and home fries would give her. Being in this diner also helped. Greek-owned diners were a neighborhood staple just about everywhere in Manhattan. There was a uniformity about them, especially in the way they smelled, as if they all brewed their soup in the same communal pot each morning. That kind of reliability felt good to Delia right now. The only thing out of the ordinary were the signs of the season, carols playing in the background and colored lights strung along the wall shelf behind the counter. Unfortunately, their off and on twinkle reminded her of Penelope Wren's living room.

Delia turned away from that reminder. Nick sat watching her from across the table while his coffee cooled in front of him. His expression was very perplexed, as if he might be watching a bomb that might or might not explode. His bewilderment struck her as very funny somehow. Despite all the horrendous things that had been happening to her and around her, maybe in defiance of them, she began to laugh. The sound was almost foreign to her at first. She hadn't heard herself laugh in what felt like an extremely long time. She hadn't thought about it till this minute, but she really hadn't laughed much in general over the past five years. That realization made part of her want to stop laughing and start crying, but she didn't.

"Are you all right?"

The very tentative way he asked that, as though he saw her as an eggshell so fragile even a raise in his voice could collapse her shell, sent her into another gale of laughter more irrepressible than the first. She tried to choke it back, but there was no stopping the peals of what sounded like merriment trilling through her and out of her. The other patrons of the diner looked quizzically her way. She took a deep breath and clamped her mouth shut. Several more small eruptions burst through the bulwark, but they were considerably reserved compared to the uncontrolled guffawing of a moment ago. She kept herself staring at the Formica table in front of her. She wasn't ready to look at Nick just yet. She was certain she'd be set off into further paroxysms if she did.

"Delia, are you all right? Can you talk to me?"

Two questions at once. Oh, no! She nodded yes to the first and shook her head no to the second. The absurdity of that was more than she could stand. She burst out giggling this time, like she couldn't remember herself doing since her teenage pajama party days. She knew she had to stop this and get back under control. She was close to gasping for breath. She bent over, put her forehead on the table and tried to focus on the coolness of the Formica-topped surface while sporadic spasms continued to escape then began gradually to subside.

She said a small, silent prayer that she would be able to pull herself together and stay that way. When she finally thought it was safe to lift her head, she found the waiter standing by the table with a full plate of food held just a few inches above where her head had been on the table. She clamped her teeth down hard on her lower lip.

"She's remembering something funny," Nick said, and Delia had to bite her lip even harder.

The waiter looked at her, shrugged, then set the plate down in front of her. "No matter," he said. "In New York I see everything."

Fortunately for Delia's struggle toward decorum, he walked away after that. She gulped in another deep breath, then another.

"Oh, dear, oh, dear, oh, dear," she chanted as she resolved to compose herself right this very minute. Nick was still watching her and still perplexed. She could feel that without looking at him. "I'm all right," she managed in a voice quavering on the edge of her hard-fought-for control. "Just a little tension release, I guess."

She inhaled deeply and let her breath out slowly each time. The yoga class she'd taken a couple of years ago was coming in handy now.

"I can think of worse ways of getting rid of stress," he said, sounding relieved.

She looked up at him then, at his dark, shadowed eyes and the tumble of thick hair blown thicker still by the winter wind. Suddenly the impulse to laugh had disappeared.

"I can think of a better way," she said.

Her near whisper carried with it a charge of sexual energy that crackled across the table. She saw Nick suck in his breath fast and knew the charge had connected.

"I think we'd better stick to the business at hand for the moment," he said after a few deep breaths of his own.

An image of the two of them together on top of this table flashed across Delia's mind. They were tearing each other's clothes off while plates and cutlery crashed to the floor around them. She felt her pulse race and had to gasp again. First a spastic fit of laughter, now vivid turn-on fantasies. She absolutely had to get a grip on herself.

"And what is the business at hand?" she forced herself to ask. She was still shaky.

"Well, to start with, I don't believe Samuel lives in that apartment we were just in," Nick said as he continued to eye her warily.

"What makes you say that?"

Nick leaned so close across the table she could smell his clean, masculine scent. Delia had to will herself to concentrate on what he was saying.

"Samuel was a nut for nature, so much so I can't imagine he isn't still into it. He collected pieces of wood and stones he thought had interesting shapes. He kept a lot of plants, too. He had a natural talent for making them grow, and he loved to take care of them. There were no plants or nature specimens in what we saw of that apartment, and I'm willing to wager there are none in the rest of it, either."

"Maybe he lost interest in that stuff."

"Maybe, except that it was more than an interest with Samuel. It was his passion."

Nick was still leaning close, watching her. He probably could see skepticism in her eyes.

"Do you have that letter?" he asked.

"What?" She didn't get what he was talking about right away.

"The letter we found at Penelope's that was supposed to have come from Samuel."

She thought for a moment, then reached into the pocket of her coat, which she'd flung over the booth back next to her. She took out the crumpled envelope.

"Here it is," she said.

Nick took the envelope out of her hand and looked it over.

"See," he said. "Just like I thought I remembered. The return address isn't written out in longhand like the rest. It's just a printed label. There are stationery stores and office places in this town that will stamp these things out for you while you wait. Anybody could have had this label made and put it on here to look like Samuel was living at that address."

Delia snorted and shook her head. "You're really desperate to come up with a way to make it look like my brother isn't behind this thing, aren't you?"

Nick had his mouth open and a look on his face that made her almost certain he was about to launch into a defense of his theory when the front door to the diner burst open and a hefty guy in a bright green down parka charged in.

"Happy Christmas Eve day, everybody," he shouted.

The cashier by the door smiled wryly. "Same to you, Jimmy," she said.

Delia shot up out of the booth and grabbed her coat, nearly sweeping the plate of untouched breakfast off the table.

"I have to go," she said. "There's something I promised to do today, and I have to do it."

How could she have lost track of such an important occasion as Christmas Eve day? She really had been taken out of herself by all that'd been happening to her lately.

"You can come along if you like," she said to Nick, who was still sitting in the booth with his mouth open.

She turned on her heel and headed for the door almost too quickly to let herself think that he just might be right about the envelope.

ONE OF THE LAST places Nick wanted them to head for right now was Hester Street. He'd argued with Delia about that half the way down there, including through the stop at Gramercy Park, which he also didn't want to make. Then he gave up. He'd always thought of himself as a persuasive man, but he was no match for her stubbornness. She insisted she had obligations and refused to listen to his objections, and that was that. He'd never known a woman, or maybe anybody at all, who could make him so exasperated. The last time she was in this neighborhood, somebody tried to run her over with a car. What could she be in for now? Maybe a sniper out to shoot her in the head? That thought, and the way it rang through to Nick as a real possibility, sent his hand to the back of his waistband to assure himself his hardware was still there and at the ready.

Delia came across as a piece of hardware herself sometimes, like now when she was determined to have things her own way. She also still believed Samuel could be behind all of this. Her insistence on that almost had Nick considering the possibility she could be right. At least, Samuel might be one of the possible suspects, along with Tobias Wren, who appeared to have dropped out of sight. There was also the not-so-incredible theory that Delia's tormentor came from right here on Hester Street. A smart woman like her should know that could be true, but she didn't want to hear about it. Nick, on the other hand, was well aware that this settlement house was full of repeat offenders, substance abusers and, most significantly, people who were down on their luck and close to desperate. That added up to strong motive in Nick's book.

"Motive for what?" Delia asked.

They were on their way up the steps to the front door of the settlement house main building. They'd been at the diner during late lunch hour, even though they'd ordered breakfast. The ride down here with a stop in between had taken nearly two hours. It was now going on the end of afternoon. The sky was already turning dark, maybe with the chance of more snow. The lights had been turned on over the door. Two fellows were on ladders on each side of the doorway, stringing lights and garland. Nick's guess was that they'd deliberately waited till Christmas Eve, the last minute, to do the outdoor decorating. Otherwise in a neighborhood like this one, the decorations were liable to get stolen before the holiday came around.

"Motive for knocking over a lady from uptown and picking her pockets clean," he said in answer to Delia.

"Who do you think would do that?"

Another naive question. Nick sighed. "Jaycee and her friends are one possibility."

"And where do you think she parks her late-model sedan while she's living on the streets?"

Delia had a point. Jaycee and her gang weren't likely to own a car like the one that tried to run Delia down. Still, there were other possibilities.

"People like this sell information all the time. Maybe whoever's after you got to somebody here and put them on the payroll."

Nick had opened the front door for Delia to pass through. When he looked up, he noticed the guys on the ladder were giving him the evil eye. They must have heard what he said. He told himself he didn't care. He knew he had a cop's suspicion of street people and the like. Though he knew that was a prejudice, he also believed he was justified in thinking the way he did. That's why he checked up and down the street for lurking characters, and vehicles, too, before following Delia inside. He avoided the hostile stares of the guys on the ladders. They'd probably made him for a cop type by now. That meant he and they were natural enemies, or at least on opposite sides of a very important line. Nick felt like telling them that he liked being on Hester Street even less than they wanted him here, but he kept his mouth shut.

Delia didn't head left toward the classrooms as she had the other day. She turned right along a wide corridor where kids were draping handmade paper chains over the tops of the bulletin boards and in doorways. For a moment the red and green construction paper loops strung together reminded Nick of his own childhood. He was a little surprised to see they still made paper chains. Some things about holiday time and kids must stay the same always. He reminded himself not to get too nostalgic about that.

The activity in the corridor grew even more intense as they approached a wide doorway. Delia pushed the

latch bar on one of the double doors and hurried
through. Once again she was bustling along too fast to
let Nick move in front at point position where he could
check out what she might be getting herself into. He had
to content himself with rear guard for now, with
checking the corridor before following her through the
double doors. He was almost disgruntled to see a totally unthreatening scene of children and adults alike
scurrying about in preparation for Christmas. But, no
matter how innocent this place might appear on the
surface, he intended to keep on his toes. With that resolve in mind, he wasn't too pleased to find Delia inside the settlement house's huge recreation hall nearly
engulfed by a hug from Jaycee.

The hall was as busy as the corridor had been. Red
and green crepe paper streamers had been strung in a
canopy over rows of long tables covered with white paper tablecloths decorated with children's holiday draw-
ings in crayon. As he strode past one of those tables,
Nick recognized the same kind of stick figure family
he'd drawn himself as a child. The mother, father and
children were holding hands between a Christmas tree
and a fireplace with stockings hung at the mantel. Nick
wondered how many of the children who came to this
place had ever actually experienced such an idyllic scene
in their own lives. The thought couldn't help but touch
his heart with a pang of compassion. All the same, he
hurried across the rec hall toward Delia.

They'd stopped at Gramercy Park on the way down
here so she could pick up a huge bag of gifts she'd
stashed in her apartment. Nick had been dead set
against doing that, but once again she wouldn't listen.
His frustration level had been over the top from then
on. When she'd insisted on carrying the bag of gifts

herself, he'd shrugged and let her do it. Now, Jaycee was directing Delia toward the evergreen tree at the other end of the hall. She hurried toward it with Jaycee in her wake and Nick not far behind but at enough of a distance so he could survey the room and Delia at the same time.

She unloaded a pile of brightly wrapped packages and arranged them under the tree that was hung with more paper chains and strings of popcorn, too. In fact, all of the decorations on the tree looked to be hand-made. Nick couldn't help remembering the elaborate trees in the lobby of the Waldorf-Astoria and thinking how much more like a real Christmas this one here looked. There he was, in danger once again of turning to holiday mush, until a glimpse of Delia's face rehardened his resolve.

Jaycee had been poking around among the tree branches while the pile of gifts was being stacked underneath. Finally, she'd pulled an envelope out, the square kind that holiday cards come in. She handed the envelope to Delia. Nick was instantly reminded of the card she'd picked up at her mail service office and what turned out to be written inside. He watched as she slipped her finger under the envelope flap and tore it open. He'd been right. It was a card. She didn't appear to pay much attention to what was on the outside. She flipped the card open almost instantly and read what was inside. It was his glimpse of her face at that moment that sent Nick hurrying toward her.

"What is it?" he asked, trying to keep his voice calmer than he was feeling.

She swept past him, shaking her head as if to indicate that she couldn't answer right now as she headed toward the door out of the recreation hall.

"Where are you going?" he called after her, taking long strides to keep up with her near-run.

Once again she didn't answer. They were outside the settlement house, down Hester Street and into yet another taxi before Nick found out that they were headed back uptown.

Chapter Twenty-One

All Delia could think about was getting this over with. The card promised that. "Meet me tonight," it said, "and all will be revealed. No police, or you're the one they will be taking away." The scrawl could be Samuel's, or somebody trying to make her think it was Samuel. She didn't know which it might be. Right now she wasn't even sure she cared. She just wanted the tension to be finished, no more hiding out or being chased or running from one place to the next to keep from being found out. Her life had to settle itself, one way or the other. Either she'd be free at last or on her way to prison or maybe even dead. Whatever happened, she had to find some measure of peace. Something told her that following the instructions on this latest card would allow her that.

She had mixed feelings about dragging Nick along for this last act. After all, she didn't know what the ending would be. If she was on her way to inevitable defeat, she didn't want him to suffer that fate with her. Whatever doubts she might have about a future with him, she cared very much about his safety and happiness. She cared very much about him in general. She wouldn't want anything to hurt him ever, especially not because of her. On the other hand, she wasn't too proud to admit she was frightened of what might lie ahead tonight, and after tonight, as well. She needed Nick, by her side and on her side, and she knew it. There was no getting rid of him anyway. He'd attached himself to her like a shadow. That was his job for now. She would have liked to think about whether or not that attachment might last beyond this bodyguard assignment, but there wasn't time for that. She told the cabdriver to let them off at West End Avenue between Sixty-third and Sixty-fourth streets, as the note on the card had directed.

"What are we doing here?" Nick asked.

He'd tried to get her to answer his questions during the ride uptown, but she'd only shaken her head at him and stared out the window till he stopped asking. She felt she did owe him an answer now.

"We're getting to the bottom of things," she said.

"Could you be more specific?"

Nick had paid the cabbie who then sped immediately away. This was not a neighborhood to hang around in after dark despite attempts to gentrify the area with an upscale high-rise apartment building and a park in the next block. The vacant lot in front of them was desolate and dark except for some spillover light from lamps in the small park. Even that light was obscured by the huge tufts of snow that had begun falling as Delia and Nick traveled from Hester Street.

"How long is this silent treatment going to last?" Nick asked when she didn't respond to his previous question.

Was that what he thought she was doing? Freezing him out with silence? Maybe he was right, though she longed to fly into his arms. She'd clasp him close to whisper, "My darling, my sweet darling," in his ear and

pray for those tremulous words to convey everything—
her years of loneliness, her limbo life between Rebecca
Lester and Delia Barry, her desperate need to have all of
that ended once and forever. What she uttered instead
was much less expressive but all she could manage at the
moment.

"Everything will be revealed," she said quietly.

"What?"

She spoke louder. "The card from Hester Street said
all would be revealed if I came to this place tonight."

"Here?"

Nick looked up and down the block. There wasn't a
soul in sight.

"Here," Delia said, and headed into the vacant lot.
She'd made it only a few steps before Nick grabbed her
arm.

"Do you know how crazy this is?" he demanded.

"Please, don't shout at me."

"I'm sorry."

He sounded desperate and kept his grip on her arm.
She wished she could explain her own desperation. She
hadn't the heart for that now. She had to save all of
herself for whatever awaited her beyond this empty lot.
She started walking again. For a moment he managed
to prevent her from moving out of his arm's reach, but
she continued to strain against that.

"You have to have your way, don't you," he said.

"In this, yes." She strained harder.

"If I don't let you walk into this trap now, then you'll
walk into the next one without me."

"That's right," she said.

His grip hadn't loosened, not even from her tugging
at it with all her strength. Still she had the feeling she
was close to prevailing, at least for now. A few seconds

later that proved true. Nick shrugged and released her arm.

"You might as well go ahead, then," he said. "At least I'm with you now."

She longed to tell him that having him with her was all she really wanted, but she only nodded. This time, as she began walking again, Nick was at her side. He still hadn't let go of her arm.

"Where are we, anyway?" he asked. "Do you know?"

"Vaguely," she said. "We're headed into what used to be a train yard."

"An abandoned rail yard. That sounds just perfect," Nick said in a sarcastic tone.

Delia had no defense to offer against the obvious foolhardiness of what she was doing. She simply walked on with Nick beside her and wished for two things—that her life as she'd lived it these past five alienated years would be history at last and that Nick wouldn't be hurt in the bargain. They were well into the deserted lot now, past the back edge of the adjacent park and picking their way among snow-covered mounds of heaven knew what. A figure emerged from the snowy veil of deepening darkness. Delia couldn't tell who it might be, or even if it was a man or a woman, until he turned on the flashlight in his hand and pointed it upward beneath his chin.

He'd looked scary enough in the stairwell of the Waldorf with his eyes blazing crazily down at her. He'd chilled her heart again earlier today, the way he'd gritted his teeth and snarled at Nick as they'd struggled for the gun in that apartment that might or might not have been her brother's. However frightening this man had been those other times, he was much more so now as the flashlight beam cast his sneering face in eerie shadows and ghostly light.

Nick slipped a step backward and slightly behind Delia. She might have been surprised that he didn't jump in front to shield her instead, but she could feel him reaching behind him for his gun while her body kept the man with the flashlight from seeing what was going on. Then the light beam was suddenly full on Nick and Delia. She blinked and raised her arm as if to ward off the blinding brightness. Actually, she intended that movement to be a distraction from what Nick was doing.

"Drop it, Avery."

The female voice came from behind them. Delia had heard it before. She was almost certain of that, but she couldn't place where. She turned to look over her shoulder.

"Eyes front and hands up, both of you," the voice barked. "You'll see me soon enough."

"Do you want me to give you my gun or put up my hands? I can't do both."

Delia guessed that Nick was stalling for time. His mind had to be spinning as fast as hers in search of a way out of this mess she'd walked them into. An armed maniac in front of them, a woman barking orders behind them and Nick about to lose his only weapon. Delia wished she'd given him time to find that second gun before she'd raced them off Riverside Drive.

"Put up your hands, and I'll get the gun," the woman was saying as Delia felt Nick move ever so slightly. She readied herself to follow his lead.

"None of that, smart guy."

A thud accompanied the voice this time, and Nick groaned as he fell to the ground. Delia clamped her hand over her mouth to stop her scream. The woman behind them had struck Nick with something hard enough to knock him out. Delia bent to help him.

"Stay where you are," the woman growled, setting off that flicker of memory in Delia's brain once more. "I never did trust Mr. Avery. He was always too much of a white knight for his own good."

She knew Nick. The flicker of memory grew stronger.

"I never trusted you, either, Rebecca. Or should I call you Delia?" The woman stepped around from behind, but it was too dark to see her clearly. "Put some light on the subject, Max. Miss Delia, Rebecca, whatever her name may be, is dying to see who I am. Or pretty close to dying, that is."

Max, the man with the crazy eyes, moved forward a few feet and directed the flashlight beam on the face of the woman standing in front of Delia. She studied that face—attractive, even-featured, maybe too much so. Delia still couldn't make the connection.

"You're not the only one who can make herself over," the mystery woman said. "Except that I made some more extensive changes. It's amazing what a good plastic surgeon can do."

She laughed then, and the memory chips clicked together for Delia at last.

"Cassandra?" she asked.

"Speaking of people who are close to dying. I'm supposed to have been dead for going on nine years now."

Delia was still having difficulty figuring out what was going on. "But you were in the helicopter with my father."

"Obviously, I wasn't."

"They found your body in the wreckage."

"They found *a* body. Same height, approximately the same build and age. Easy enough to find on the same streets I was wandering before your dear daddy decided to rescue me."

More memories slid into place. There'd been rumors all those years ago about Edward Lester's much younger bride. Delia hadn't paid much attention. She'd only cared that her father was happy, and devoting himself to Cassandra seemed to make him so.

"You probably heard Tobias and Penelope talking about me," this new version of Cassandra went on. Her voice was full and confident, even commanding, nothing like the timid young thing Delia remembered. "The Wrens didn't approve of me. They thought I was only out for what I could get. They were right, of course."

Delia fought to think her way through the confusion.

"It was a fair trade actually," Cassandra said. "Your father got a protégé to mold into his version of the perfect woman. There was no chance of his ever being able to do that with his darling daughter. You were too headstrong. I, on the other hand, was more than willing to be molded. I was nobody going nowhere when he came along. He taught me everything I needed to know to become somebody. How to dress, what to read, what to like, even what to think."

A corner of the picture began to come clearer for Delia. The portraits on that living room wall this morning. The study that looked so much like her father's.

"That's your apartment up on Riverside Drive, isn't it?" she said.

"Good for you. You're starting to put it together."

More of the picture grew clear for Delia, none of it too savory.

"Did you kill Penelope Wren?" Delia asked.

"Good for you again." Cassandra poked Delia in the chest with the barrel of the gun she was holding. "I took care of them all, or to be precise, I had Max do it. You've met Max, haven't you? We've been together from way back in my street days. We're quite a team. I do most of his talking for him. He does all of my dirty work for me."

"What do you mean, you took care of them all?" Delia asked as the horror of what the answer might be crept into her bones.

"I had Max kill everybody I needed to be rid of," Cassandra said. If her voice hadn't been so cold, she might have sounded gleeful. "Penelope and Tobias, Morty Lancer and, of course, your father."

Delia sobbed once then lunged forward, grabbing Cassandra who hopped out of the way and toppled down. She must have tripped over something under the snow. Delia was on top of her in an instant.

"You killed my father," Delia cried. "You killed my father."

Her heart was breaking and exploding with rage, both at the same moment. She pounded her fists into Cassandra wherever contact could be made. Delia was oblivious of the gun. All she could think of was that her world had been destroyed, and her precious father along with it, because of this woman. Delia couldn't keep herself from giving back some of that pain now. One of them probably would have ended up dead or at least unconscious if Max hadn't dragged Delia away and tossed her into the snow next to Nick, who groaned and stirred then was still again. What could he do anyway?

Max stood over them with a gun and the flashlight. Cassandra picked herself up and brushed the snow off her coat. Then she was standing there pointing a gun at Nick and Delia, too.

"Why?" Delia asked. "Why have you done all of this?"

Cassandra laughed. "The money, of course. But you wouldn't understand that, would you? A pampered little rich girl like you wouldn't have any idea what it's like to have nothing or how far a person might go to change that."

Delia could hear the hatred behind Cassandra's taunting. Had she been this way before, when they'd lived in the same house back in Colorado? Delia wished she'd paid more than passing attention to her stepmother back then.

"How did you find me?" Delia asked.

"That precious ring of yours. Your daddy told me the whole touching story of your mother giving it to you on her deathbed. Your daddy told me everything, even that silly name he called you. Topsy. Isn't that just too, too dear?"

There was envy behind Cassandra's sneer, along with the hatred, powerful enough emotions to fuel her murderous rage. Delia could see that now.

"I'm surprised that my father shared those things with you," she said.

"I could make your daddy tell me anything. The only one easier to get to than him was Morty Lancer. Of course, he wanted his cut of the money, too. That's how I got him to rig the will. He was siphoning off his own cut in the meantime, but I knew that and he knew I knew it."

"Did Morty know you weren't in the crash?"

"He wasn't smart enough to figure that out, any more than he was smart enough to steal small. That's why I had to get rid of him finally. He was a greedy little man. Of course, I was too smart for him. Even before your darling daddy died, I'd diverted lots of money and securities into the trust fund accounts with a holding company in control. I controlled the holding company under what I'd already set up to be my new name and identity. Then he got greedy. Unfortunately we couldn't get straight to the money even with Morty pulling the strings. We had to go the trust fund route to not be caught. You were too much of an airhead to pay attention to what was going on, your brother was too crazy to care, and Morty was the sole trustee. It was a perfect setup till good old Morty pushed his pilfering too far. If I hadn't stopped him, he'd have bled those trust funds dry. He'd already made a dent in Samuel's."

"Samuel." Delia had been half reclining in the snow with her arm raised to keep the large flakes of snow out of her face. She shot up now into a crouch that brought Max's gun directly to the side of her head. "What have you done to Samuel? Did you kill him, too?"

Cassandra laughed again, even more cruelly. "Why would I need to do that? He's too harmless to bother with. Besides, he's been useful to me. I did have him moved to another institution, just in case you ever decided to go after him and started checking his finances too closely. Of course, you never did."

Delia felt a twinge of guilt more chilling than the wet gradually seeping through her jeans.

"How did you manage moving him? Don't papers have to be signed?"

"A lawyer, silly girl. It's always possible to find a crooked one of those. This time I was smart enough to buy one smarter than Morty Lancer. His partner, in fact, a natural to take over the Lester estate work. He thinks I'm a distant relative of your father's just as Morty did. But then, neither of them ever questioned my story very closely. Morty was too busy grabbing up the money I let him embezzle, and his partner has enough brains to know he should keep his mouth shut. Anyway, everything's run like clockwork since Morty died. Morty was a loose end, so I snipped him off. Putting him in your bed just tied things up, nice and neat. I like things neat. Then you took off and spoiled everything. But I had a feeling you'd show up again someday.

"Then the other day, there you were, big as life in Saks Fifth Avenue of all places, right across the counter from me. I'd call it fate. I'd told myself I'd run into you someday and get rid of you like all the rest. You might never figure out what was going on, but maybe you would. That's a chance I wouldn't want to take. So, fate brought you to me, fate and a little luck, good luck for me, bad for you, just like what's going to happen to you and Avery now."

Cassandra stepped back. Unfortunately she didn't trip this time.

"Time to get on with it," she said. "Right, Max? Now that I've made sure the poor little rich girl knows how the kid from the gutter outsmarted the whole Lester clan and ended up on Easy Street."

Nick stirred again next to Delia, then rolled over. She reached for his arm.

"How sweet," Cassandra said, "and better for Max, too. He likes to have his victims see what they've got coming to them."

Max's eyes glinted, more insane than ever in the beam from the flashlight, but that wasn't what had Delia's attention at the moment. Forms were moving out of the darkness behind Cassandra and Max, advancing toward them without sound through the muffling snow. At first Delia thought Cassandra might have enlisted more henchmen, but that didn't make sense. Why would she need anybody besides herself and Max and their minimum of two firearms?

These new arrivals were decidedly bedraggled. Delia could see that more and more clearly as they entered the peripheral glow of the flashlight. Suddenly, Delia remembered where she was. This abandoned rail yard was exactly the kind of place that attracted the homeless, both good and bad, as a squatting ground. Delia's stomach clenched. It looked like she and Nick had more than just Cassandra and her crazy sidekick to contend with.

Delia watched the leader of the ragged band move into view behind Max and coiled herself to spring to the attack, as she was certain Nick must also be doing next to her. Then she saw the leader's face glaring purposefully from beneath a Santa Claus hat fringed in wild, frizzy gray hair.

Jaycee! Delia wanted to cry out.

But there were no greetings in that abandoned rail yard, not until the sounds of scuffling died down and Max and Cassandra had been disarmed by the Hester Street gang with Nick joining in. Then Jaycee came

forward wearing her crooked grin and reached her hand
out toward Delia.

"Merry Christmas, sugar," Jaycee said.

JAYCEE HAD PREDICTED two gifts for Delia that
Christmas Eve. The first, from Jaycee herself, was de-
liverance from becoming yet another of Cassandra's
victims. Jaycee had used what Delia had taught her to
read that Christmas card over her shoulder back at the
settlement house. Jaycee guessed there was big trouble
in store when she saw the look on Nick's face as he
scurried out of there after Delia. Jaycee went into action then, mobilizing everybody at the center, com-
mandeering one of the trucks waiting to be loaded with
Christmas dinners for needy families.

The rest was history—the end of the story for Cassandra and Max, the beginning for Delia and Nick who
spent the next several hours on that same truck helping
deliver those dinners and belting out carols at the top of
their lungs till they were hoarse from song and laughter. There'd be time to clear everything up with the police later on. Until then, this was the first Christmas of
their new life together, and neither of them intended to
miss a single, blessed, beautiful minute of it.

"The second gift Jaycee promised," Delia whispered as she and Nick tumbled up to her apartment
door, arms around each other and near exhaustion.

"What are you talking about?" Nick asked.

Delia pointed to the package leaning against the door.

"I have a feeling this is the gift from heaven in Jaycee's vision."

Nick laughed, and it was the happiest sound she'd ever heard. "Then you'd better open it," he said, and bent to kiss her, sweet as Christmas candy, full on the lips.

Delia kissed him back and held him very tight for a moment.

"Let's go inside first," she said.

Christmas morning was dawning behind the blinds in Delia's living room. She hurried to the window and pulled the cord to let that light into the room.

"No need to hide anymore," she said. "That's all over."

"Yes, it is," Nick answered, taking her coat.

She smiled and sighed, as if his agreement made the words suddenly true and put the years of fear and subterfuge behind her for certain and for good. She sat down on the floor next to the blue spruce and unwrapped the brown paper from the package she'd discovered outside her door. She recognized what she found inside the moment she saw it, and a gasp escaped her lips as she choked back her tears. Cassandra had mentioned leaving Delia a second, even more enticing invitation to the rail yard, in case she didn't get the one at Hester Street. Here it was, the linen-covered book Delia remembered so well.

"What is it?" Nick asked.

"My father's journal," she said.

She ran her fingers over the faded cover. She would save the reading of it for later on. She understood that what her father had written here would restore him to her in a way nothing else could have done. This book was exactly what Jaycee had predicted.

"A gift from heaven," Delia murmured again.

Nick knelt beside her, and she lifted her face to his as they wound their arms around each other. "You're a gift from heaven," he said.

"Merry Christmas, my love," Delia whispered in response as she gazed at the spun glass angel sparkling from a blue spruce branch and held Nick tight.

HARLEQUIN®
I N T R I G U E®

In steamy New Orleans, three women witnessed the same crime, testified against the same man and were then swept into the Witness Protection Program. But now, there's new evidence. These three women are about to come out of hiding—and find both danger and desire....

Start your new year right with all the books in the exciting EYEWITNESS miniseries:

#399 A CHRISTMAS KISS
by Caroline Burnes (December)

#402 A NEW YEAR'S CONVICTION
by Cassie Miles (January)

#406 A VALENTINE HOSTAGE
by Dawn Stewardson (February)

Don't miss these three books—or miss out on all the passion and drama of the crime of the century!

Take 4 bestselling love stories FREE

Plus get a FREE surprise gift!

Ring in the New Year with babies, families and romance!

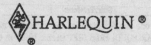

Free Gift Offer

With a Free Gift proof-of-purchase
from any Harlequin® book, you can receive
a beautiful cubic zirconia pendant.

This stunning marquise-shaped stone is a genuine cubic
zirconia—accented by an 18" gold tone necklace.
(Approximate retail value $19.95)

Send for yours today...

compliments of ✿HARLEQUIN®

To receive your free gift, a cubic zirconia pendant, send us one original proof-of-
purchase, photocopies not accepted, from the back of any Harlequin Romance®,
Harlequin Presents®, Harlequin Temptation®, Harlequin Superromance®, Harlequin
Intrigue®, Harlequin American Romance®, or Harlequin Historicals® title available in
August, September or October at your favorite retail outlet, together with the Free Gift
Certificate, plus a check or money order for $1.65 U.S./$2.15 CAN. (do not send cash) to
cover postage and handling, payable to Harlequin Free Gift Offer. We will send you the
specified gift. Allow 6 to 8 weeks for delivery. Offer good until December 31, 1996, or
while quantities last. Offer valid in the U.S. and Canada only.

Free Gift Certificate

Name: _____

Address: _____

City: _____ State/Province: _____ Zip/Postal Code: _____

Mail this certificate, one proof-of-purchase and a check or money order for postage
and handling to: HARLEQUIN FREE GIFT OFFER 1996. In the U.S.: 3010 Walden
Avenue, P.O. Box 9071, Buffalo NY 14269-9057. In Canada: P.O. Box 604, Fort Erie,
Ontario L2Z 5X3.

FREE GIFT OFFER   084-KMFR

ONE PROOF-OF-PURCHASE
To collect your fabulous FREE GIFT, a cubic zirconia pendant, you must include this
original proof-of-purchase for each gift with the properly completed Free Gift Certificate.

084-KMFR

1997
Reader's Engagement Book
A calendar of important dates
and anniversaries for readers to use!

Informative and entertaining—with notable
dates and trivia highlighted throughout the year.

Handy, convenient, pocketbook size to help you
keep track of your own personal important dates.

Added bonus—contains $5.00 worth of coupons
for upcoming Harlequin and Silhouette books.
This calendar more than pays for itself!

Available beginning in November at
your favorite retail outlet.

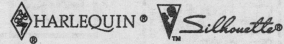

You're About to Become a *Privileged Woman*

Reap the rewards of fabulous free gifts and benefits with proofs-of-purchase from Harlequin and Silhouette books

Pages & Privileges™

It's our way of thanking you for buying our books at your favorite retail stores.

✂

PROOF OF PURCHASE
Offer expires March 31, 1997

HI-PP20

**Harlequin and Silhouette—
the most privileged readers in the world!**

For more information about Harlequin and Silhouette's PAGES & PRIVILEGES program call the Pages & Privileges Benefits Desk: 1-503-794-2499

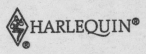 HARLEQUIN®

HI-PP20